The Cry of the Humble

The Cry of the Humble

Vignettes from a Life Well Lived

Paul W. Lavender

Edited by Judi Thompson

Blackmore & Blackmore
Portland, Oregon

Previously Published in 1982
by J.G. Blaeschke Verlag
Printed in Austria

Book Design by Judi Thompson
Cover Artwork by Stefan Bercs

ISBN 0-9666244-0-8

Blackmore & Blackmore
117 N.W. Trinity Place, Suite C
Portland, Oregon 97209
USA
Tel (503) 228-6422
Fax (503) 228-9680

To my wife,
Edith

He hath not forgotten
the cry of the humble

Psalm 9:12

Contents

Part V – Religion

Part VI – Mankind

Part VII – Novella

* * *

We have only a vague idea of
where we come from
We have no knowledge of
where we go
However we have means of finding out
where we stand

Preface

This book contains "vignettes" written throughout the lifetime of the author. They are presented here in book form in order to create a legible collection of these writings, many of which were mimeographed before the advent of the modern duplicating machine. These lines are truly vignettes of life: thoughts, opinions, situations, humor and dead-seriousness. Some of them may seem antiquated. It is amazing what changes take place in the span of forty years. This fact alone might add rather than detract from the contents. As vignettes are short literary compositions with no definite confines, the reader may find similar thoughts expressed in connection with different subjects, an on-going thread as these ideas were spread over such a long period of time.

My wife, Edith, and I immigrated to the United States of America in the year 1937, coming from Germany via a four-year stay in the Netherlands, Amsterdam. Writing seems to be a family trait as my brother, Dr. Herbert Lewandowski (also known as Lee van Dovski), is a writer by profession. His works are well known throughout Europe.

I have written purely for my own enjoyment, not with the intent to commercialize these thoughts.

Paul W. Lavender

Part I
My Life

Autobiography

This section of the book is an autobiography of the author, depicting his life from the beginning until the time he arrives on the shores of the United States of America and his first impressions until the end of World War II. The lines were taken from a scrapbook, written and added to at various times.

The shortest word ever found for the longest, most grueling occupation of mankind is "WAR." I have the feeling that war is an abbreviation for "Waylaying Another Rascal."

When I was only three years old, World War I broke out. The war was lost alright by Germany, but the victory songs that had been taught to us in school for many weeks were presented in spite of it. I can still visualize myself standing in the first row of the school choir, singing to hundreds of returning soldiers passing by who were too tired even to listen. Their real welcome-home salute was given by the men cutting the insignias of rank from the uniforms of every soldier, thus putting them all in the same class. I also remember the mob, breaking shop windows, putting the more valuable objects into their pockets while throwing the rest into the street. That was the day of revolution in 1918. The downtown district looked like the morning after a carnival. When order could not be restored in a normal fashion, barricades were thrown up and certain districts isolated through which one could not pass without a permit.

In those years during and after the war, we ate margarine instead of butter, existed on the most rudimentary types of meat and sweetened our lives with saccharine instead of sugar. Somehow we lived through this period of time during which my character was formed. In a way, this mode of life was advantageous to the young; we learned how to appreciate things.

School did not make my life more enjoyable, which it should have done. New things are supposed to awaken interest and keep the mind on the alert. The teachers, however, showed partiality toward their pets and hatred toward Jewish children.

I liked to learn the foreign languages they taught: French, English and Latin. Later, I took up Spanish in night-school and Dutch in the hard day-school of making a living in Holland.

I began to have fun after joining a club which we would call a scout club here in America. Almost every Sunday, we would wander into the nearby mountains, play ball, sing, swim and have discussions. There I got acquainted with the conflicts among the Jews, the Nationalists (Central Verein) and the Zionists. During vacations, we would make trips lasting as long as a week or two. Once a year the climax was the "Bundestag" or general assembly to which Jewish youth from all over Germany would come and we would sleep in barnyards, above pig stables or on dancing floors. Our belongings were packed in a knapsack or an old army tournister (Affe). Sometimes I would be detailed to carry the "big pot," in which we cooked rice, tasting more like little stones. Wherever we could find youth hostels, we made use of them. When we did not walk, we talked. There was much ground to cover and our conversational scope was wide.

Time went on and school days passed. Learning applied means earning. I entered as an apprentice at Leonhard Tietz, then the greatest department store chain in Germany. The president of the store suggested to my father that I learn the house furnishings, glass and china trade. To quote him, "Dear Sir: The greatest future for a young man lies right there."

I still remember that first day of work so long ago. I had to load, unload and push carts all day long and this during a big housewares sale. When I came home that night, I was not able to sit, stand or lie down, so worn out did I feel. It seems, however, that I overcame these reactions. During my apprentice years, I had occasion to get fully acquainted with the entire internal workings of a department store. I wrote many articles about this subject, some of which were published in the nation-wide store paper.

My boss had two beautiful daughters, the older one being about sixteen years of age. She wrote me childish letters, which I then interpreted as love. My father would not have minded my becoming related to the president of the store, but thoughts of marriage were far from my mind then.

Slowly and surely I grew up to be what is colloquially called "a young man." My parents sent me to dancing lessons, which included courses on the principles of etiquette. Of course, only sophisticated dances like the waltz and the tango were taught. I attended ball masques and did not get half so tired dancing all night as I did when pushing carts during the day. I fell in and out of love; the more proper word would be devotion. Sometimes, I would take an affair a little more seriously than was justified, but the girls were smart enough not to let me get entangled. Of the highlights in life, romance undoubtedly shines the brightest. Romance is the last kiss blown from Paradise.

To be sensitive is justified as long as it is linked with the capability of being sensible.

Clubless since leaving the Scouts, I was drawn into an organization endeavoring to further the ties and feelings of responsibility among Jewish youth. Actually I wanted to retire from public life at the age of seventeen. I felt that the squabbles about unimportant issues were elevated to highest prominence, a condition which seemed to me utterly senseless. The real problem was the political and economical situation in which Germany found itself after the First World War and I realized that to solve these problems, one had to understand the causes underlying them. I dug deep down by studying the development from the Dawes Plan to the Young Plan. I gave a lecture series regarding this subject on three successive evenings, my talk concerning the basis upon which Germany was placed by the victorious Allies.

"The Young Plan is the best solution for Germany," I said, "giving consideration to the circumstances. This does not deny, however, that the burden of this plan which was then heavily placed upon the people and the economy of Germany does require a revision. This not only in the interests of this country, but also for the benefit of the other partners (the Allies) in order to avoid a breakdown of the world economy."

It seems that I was not too far off. Only three years later, Hitler became Reichs-Chancellor and the gruesome results are well remembered.

3

In 1931, I was transferred by the company from Kassel to their store in Wiesbaden in the capacity of Assistant Buyer for China and Glass. The move initiated new independence for me. I was away from home for the first time, exchanging parental protection for greater liberty. I realized then that this entire new chapter of my life depended solely on its author – myself. I felt that the whole world was mine. I was free at last. What use would I make of this freedom?

After one week, I was invited to attend a club affair in one of the big hotels on the famous Wilhelmstrasse, the Broadway of Wiesbaden. It was here in the city where people from all over the world would meet, seeking health in this famous spa. They would drink water from hot springs or bathe in it as the Romans had done before them. They would enjoy the beautiful surroundings and the gentle climate. At night they would wend their way to a dance, just as I did. Even though I worked in the city, I felt more like a summer guest.

At the dance I met a sweet, dainty and intelligent young lady. She danced like a feather, which made me feel as though I danced expertly too. Soon we found that our interests ran parallel. I was learning Spanish, which she was also pursuing. She loved music; so did I. We shared the same enthusiasms. In retrospect, we were products of our time. While Edith admired the beauty of nature, I was engulfed in the nature of beauty. At some memorable date, we bought each other a book as a gift. When we unwrapped the packages, we found that we had bought the same book. Far from marring the event, the coincidence held a tender significance.

Time marched on. After one year, I was promoted to the position of buyer at the Koblenz branch store. Twenty-two years of age at the time, I was the youngest buyer in an organization of more than fifty stores. Only one night before this news broke, Edith and I had made plans for the coming spring. We wanted to buy a paddle boat to travel down the River Rhine, but this idea suffered the fate of so many others in those turbulent days.

I arrived in Koblenz on January 16, 1933. Five days later, Adolph Hitler became *Reichskanzler*, a change in the leadership of the government which made itself felt on the same day. All the Nazi conspirators, hidden so far, popped their heads above ground. The change was so sudden that a stockboy in our store earnestly approached the president of the store in his office demanding his place. The fellow thought himself entitled to it merely because he was an Aryan!

Soon all large stores which were owned by Jews or employed Jews among their help, were beleaguered by Nazis, now in uniform. They tried to prevent customers from entering the stores of Jews and "foreigners." Actually the only foreigner in town, the American Woolworth Store, was not bothered.

It can well be imagined what chance I had as a buyer in such a period. The entrances of the store were barricaded most of the time, the doors often being closed altogether to prevent bloodshed when the mob seemed to reach a boiling point. Once I recall when a few loyal customers fought their way inside, a horde of twenty bandits with pistols drawn walked from floor to floor demanding that the store be cleared. I saw more than one woman rolling down the steps.

This was just the beginning of the greatest spectacle of horror, I believe, that the world has ever witnessed. Strange as it seems, the horror was so stark that even many Jews could not grasp what they saw. They were so instilled with culture, with the philosophy of Kant, the writings of Goethe and Schiller, that there seemed to be no niche into which horror like this could fall. Owners of stores were forced at gunpoint to brand reports about persecution of Jews in Germany as propaganda lies.

Inevitably, I soon found myself without a job. I was fired. It seemed a bleak day to me then, but it turned out to be the proverbial blessing in disguise.

On the seventh day of August, 1933, I reached Amsterdam, the capital of Holland. I was now what is generally classified as "a refugee." I have often wondered why few countries actually have a word of their own for a person in that dilemma. Linguists know that the French adopted the word from the Latin, *refugere,* and the Latins, I am sure, had sufficient cause to look back at the Greeks and Herbrews to whom this word was no novelty. Adam fleeing

5

from Paradise was the world's first refugee. Hunger, greed, differences in belief, color, race and nation have fathered the refugee and, short of a perfect world, he will remain part of humanity.

I had an abundance of time in which to admire the quaintness of the old canals and the gabled homes lining them. It was here where Spinoza ground his lenses, wove his thoughts and, much later, where Anne Frank's diary was found. The bread lines before "The Committee For Jodsche Fluechtelingen" bore witness that an entirely different era was born. Under the agreement with the Dutch government, the committee was to sustain the refugees but not to supply them with work as the authorities felt that this would have an adverse influence on the Dutch labor market. Disinclined to retire from life at such a young age, I refused to accept aid in favor of finding some means of income on my own. The weeks that followed produced many a dried inkwell from the flow of my applications, but to no avail; employment was out of the question.

Walking the streets one day, I saw two men advertising on their backs, "The World's Finest Razor Blades!" I stopped them and inquired about the prosperity of that type of business. A guarantee of six gulden a week and the merchandise given on consignment were enough reasons to convince me. At 9 AM on the following morning, my prospective employer informed me that he had an opening in front of the Amsterdam Railroad Station. The only security required was leaving my passport. This, next to the suit on his back, was a man's most valuable possession in Europe. Yet, I left it. Soon thereafter, I could be found (had anybody the desire to seek me out) in front of the big clock of the railroad station screaming the Dutch equivalent of "Razor blades!" Two hours passed and not a pack had lightened my burden. People leaving were in a hurry to catch the train; people returning, in no mood to delay their homecoming. Later that afternoon, a redcap, who must have come up the ranks himself, bought a pack. That evening I decided that the razor blade business was not for me. My employer was in full agreement. He cancelled the six gulden a week contract and returned my passport; however, not without a hassle.

De Gruyters, one of Holland's largest coffee and tea merchants, was advertising for a salesman in their store window. They permitted me to buy coffee and tea for resale at a discount. Figuring my cash balance on hand, I felt that I could invest in one pound of coffee and two separate ounces of tea. I went out to the suburbs and started ringing doorbells. The sound of that first bell I will never forget, nor the prayer on my lips: "I hope that nobody is home!" The door was answered by a very friendly woman who bought my pound of coffee and an ounce of tea and gave me her neighbor's name. From then on, I was in business. Bell buttons became my friends and their ring sounded heavenly now. My business not only kept me drinking, but also eating.

Life in Holland was quite different from what I was accustomed to in Germany. I lodged with a cigar maker, who rolled part of his stock at home in his three-room apartment on the fourth floor, situated on famous Calver Street. The steps which led to our abode most closely resembled a chicken ladder. I shared my bed in the alcove with another outcast; there all of us slept: host, hostess, a young child and the two boarders. At night, after accidentally kicking each other awake, we could observe the mice playing on the dusty kitchen floor floodlighted by the moon shining through the kitchen window. Our hosts, however poor and dirty, had great human hearts. They helped wherever they could and on Friday night, the traditional Jewish Sabbath eve, a delicious dinner was served.

One of my dearest possessions was a warm, heavy overcoat. More than anything else, a coat such as this gives a refugee the feeling of being able to survive the onslaught. My host had none to equal it. Whenever I stayed in, he would wear it out. He felt that I had the right to share in his meager possessions and he in mine. This was not an ideology which he had evolved, but simply the result of necessity.

Once a month I had to proceed to City Hall to renew my permit to stay in Holland. This not only interfered with my activites, but was a most nerve-wracking moment. Where was I to go were Holland to discontinue her hospitality? Since my coming, borders had hermetically closed all over the world. One of my appointments fell on a Dutch holiday and a different man handled my case. He was one of the rare people who combine bureaucracy with humanity; he issued the highly valued permanent permit. Once again, I felt part of the land that had adopted me.

After a year had passed, I was able to change my lodging; instead of two people sleeping in one bed, I now slept alone in a double bed. My new hostess was the wife of a diamond cutter. Like all Dutch women, she was an excellant cook. A human being, however, needs more than work, food and a clean shelter. Companionship is an integral part of life. The coffee and tea business had since grown to a full-fledged traveling grocery store with myself as owner, operator, delivery boy, bookkeeper, accountant and tax consultant. I needed a partner, one who could share the business with me rather than slice it. Now, I felt, was the time to call for the girl I had left behind in Germany. I wrote her a letter asking her to please come and we will share our lives. The minute I had dropped the letter in the mailbox, I felt pangs in my heart. What have you done? How can a guy like you, who hardly has his feet on the ground, undertake such a tremendous responsibility? Anyway, it was too late and my genuine love for Edith replaced the momentary doubt which had barked at me so loudly.

She responded that she was happy to join me in our future venture. We got married and became partners in life to share worry, work and happiness. It was she who pushed me out of bed onto the road in the morning and it was she who dragged me into bed at night when she found me fast asleep over my papers. Paperwork becomes part of every business, no matter how small. The growing business required more equipment and greater selection. To increase the profit (such a beautiful word, often with such shallow meaning), our processing of certain foods on our own became necessary and possible.

Freak accidents added their share of heartache and, in retrospect only, humor. My first motorized vehicle consisted of a coffin-like box with a hinged top. This was set on two wheels, while the motor and I on the saddle gave weight to the third wheel in the back. One stormy day while putt-putting around a corner across from an open field, the wind lifted the lid, tore it off the hinges and blew it twenty feet away. The re-installation of the lid now became part of the long-term installment plan of the vehicle itself.

I took a great step forward on the day when I could shift from the boxcart to a truck-like affair on three wheels. (I still could not afford the fourth wheel.) The motor and I now became housed in a covered caboose in the front with the groceries behind. One fine day, while completing a circle around a block just covered, I saw the right side of the street dotted with packages which looked like mine. The rear door had opened and with every jolt one more package had tumbled through it. Hansel and Gretel could not have been more happy to pick up their morsels!

The shadow of the Hitler menace lengthened. Those who gave him only a few months back in 1933 were left with forfeited predictions and empty hands. Most of my fellow refugees led only meager existances. Was Holland a secure place to build a nest? Looking at the map, considering the consistant rise of Hitler's strength during the years from 1933 to 1936, the technological development which had brought about planes able to fly considerable distances without refueling, my wife and I felt that Holland was not the place. We did not share the feeling that Holland was safe because it was neutral. The German Bund was active within Holland's borders; the Royal House and the press felt that they were on friendly footing with Germany. In times like these, it was so easy to be lulled into a false sense of security by fine words of neutrality and promises of peaceful co-existance, hollow words which brought death to the under-armed illusionists. Ironically, history repeats itself endlessly. We honestly believe to learn from it only to find that the same dangers have outwitted us by being masked in different costumes.

We decided to move on, this time across the Atlantic Ocean, far away from the Nazi boots.

I wrote a letter to my Aunt Martha Lavender in Pittsburgh, Pennsylvania, widow of my Uncle Max, who had changed his name from Lewandowski to Lavender. I asked for affidavits, which are legal papers by which the issuer assumes responsibility for the new immigrants. In no time, her son, Dr. Jerry Lavender, a dermatologist practicing in Cincinnati, sent me documents which we looked forward to receiving most eagerly. The nearest American consul in Holland was in Den Haag. When the date was set for our interview, we traveled there. It seemed that everyone was called but Edith and I; we had nearly given up hope when our names were finally called. "Do you plan to work in America?" was one of the most important questions. "Absolutely not!" was our answer. Had we said yes, the visa would have been refused. Countries make crazy laws with the sanest of faces.

Our family in the United States made arrangements for us to come over on a German ship because they knew the agent of the Hapag-America line. It also showed how little they really knew about the Nazi danger. Needless to say, we would not touch even a plank of a German ship with our feet. We switched onto the Cunard line, an English steamship company. My dear wife got terribly seasick, saying that she preferred jumping into the cold ocean rather than staying for a week on the steamer, be it an English or German ship. Somehow we made it across the Atlantic and the Statue of Liberty winked a greeting to us as we approached Ellis Island.

An uncle of my wife, a native of New York, greeted us at the harbor. Apparently he had never left the confines of that big city. He may have known New York, but when it came to making arrangements for us to go by train to Pittsburgh, he put us on the Baltimore-Ohio Railroad, while any worldly person would have sent us via the Pennsylvania Railroad. We arrived in Pittsburgh at the Baltimore-Ohio Railroad Station while my family was waiting at the Pennsylvania Railroad Station. Fortunately, somehow we got together.

We settled in Pittsburgh, Pennsylvania. The first few years were hard ones. I started out again at exactly the same spot that I had held ten years before: as a stock boy in a department store. Gimbel Brothers for "a better measure of value," paid me the princely salary of $15.00 a week which, however, enabled me to make a living and just that. A distant relative, great-hearted as relatives usually are, employed my wife for $12.00 a week. In return, she was permitted to put in "all hours." But, indeed, we were working, a privilege at that time. The "family" was delighted with us when we first arrived; we were a novelty. When we visited them, they would say, "Come back again." Later they seemed to add silently, "But not so soon."

It did not take me long to realize that there were two jobs for me to do. First: to give the stream of newcomers to Pittsburgh from all over Europe an opportunity to acclimatize, to Americanize. Second: to try to make the inhabitants of the land of our choice understand and realize the danger which was looming on the horizon. At that time, the majority of Americans felt that they could keep out of European affairs by a simple closing of their eyes to them. What I undertook was a hard, thankless job, but it gave me the satisfaction of paying back in a small measure for the privilege of living in America.

I became president of the Newcomers Club and headed the club paper, the *Friendship News.* My editorials were attacked from many sides and I was declared a war-monger, but I fought back hard to open the eyes of the isolationists.

Just when the world situation was at its lowest level, letters from all over would arrive from friends, relatives and strangers begging for help. One minute after twelve o'clock, after six years of pondering and hesitation, the people of Europe realized their plight. My Mother and brother, Hans, still living in Holland were also caught in the whirlpool. It was too late then for them to grasp the hand we extended.

The war was on. While England promised to help Poland (an impossibility in itself), German refugees were interned by Britain. Europe was awakened from its sleep so drastically that it seemed to point the gun against itself in the early days of the campaign.

Only five weeks after the birth of our oldest daughter, Eleonore, America entered into war with Japan and Germany. Columnists, congressmen, senators and the other wise men of this country, isolationists of the first degree, had suddenly advo-cated better preparedness for a long time. They accused

President Roosevelt of not having foreseen the dilemma. Reporters who had told the public that the gigantic national debt was our ruin suddenly could not understand why a much larger budget had not been appropriated. Housewives, who only a day before Pearl Harbor had bought a new dinner set made in Japan, raced through stores, picking up any Japanese article and trampling it with their feet.

For a few weeks the country stood behind President Franklin Delano Roosevelt like one man; labor gave non-strike pledges which it broke at leisure; industry gratefully built large plants for which the government paid and in which businessmen operated on the "cost plus" basis (which means the bigger the cost, the bigger the profits). All in all, with initial reverses, the country produced war material of an unbelievable quantity in the shortest period of time and managed to provide for the world besides. This mass production changed the scales of fortune. Hitler was out-fought and out-blitzed on all fronts.

F.D.R. (who had saved the nation twice, once from economic chaos and the second time from the hordes of the horrible Hun) did not see the results of his labor. He, like Moses, died at the gates of his endeavor.

"The war is over!" Not only for us, the living, but more so for the millions of gallant fighters on the battlefields and in the concentration and extermination camps who gave their lives. I believe it to be not more than fitting to here pay tribute to all of them for their sacrifices. Tribute also to my own mother and twin brother who, so we heard from the Red Cross, were murdered in Auschwitz and Sobibar respectively, where they had been taken from Holland in August of 1942. I bow my head to all of them who gave their very lives hoping for the creation of a more ethical world.

Peace had come. Or had it?

At this point I feel obliged to write about my rather illustrious family background, not so much of their daily lives but rather of their achievements and the political climate in which they lived.

My grandfather on my father's side was Hermann Lewandowski. This was my family name until we changed it after coming to America in 1937. My Uncle Max had changed his name to Lavender in the 1880's and we felt obligated to accept his version.

Lavender has a pleasant smell. Aunt Martha, wife of my Uncle Max, felt that we could charge things easier that way.

My grandfather had twelve children and my father was the seventh child. He was born in 1860 and I was born in 1911; in other words, he was fifty years old when I was born. My twin brother, Hans, and I were actually an afterthought.

My oldest brother, Herbert Lewandowski, who became a well-known German writer, was born in 1896. He was eighteen years of age when the First World War broke out and ripe for the draft. He suggested to my father that he take his money and move to Switzerland. He could not have mentioned anything less acceptable. "We are Germans," my father said. "Germany is our Fatherland. You do your civil duty." My brother registered and even though he had studied Greek and Latin in school, he was to take care of the horses in the stable. Fortunately, he had inherited the musical strain of the family. He entertained the soldiers by playing the piano and soon was transferred to the Entertainment Department of the military. Another interesting aspect of those days was that our parents gave him a camera, something very new then, and he became the official photographer. What could be more beautiful than the ability to send home pictures of yourself?

Herbert survived the war and joined the famous film company, Ufa (similar to Metro Goldwyn Mayer in the United States).

His co-workers soon left for America; Fritz Lang and Eric Pommer became successful movie directors there. My brother chose to stay behind. He moved to Holland in the 1920s. When the Germans marched into Holland in 1940, he fled with his family to Paris. When the Germans moved further south, he was forced to leave his family behind in Lyon. When the Germans came to arrest his son, his mother had him strip to prove that he was not Jewish. Because he was not circumcised, he was freed. Somehow, by God's will, he was taken care of. My brother walked over the Swiss mountains into Switzerland with snow and ice as his companions. Again by God's grace, he found the footsteps of the border-guard which led him straight down to a little church at the foot of the mountain. The priest helped him to get registered. Switzerland, which refused entry to many Jews, admitted intellectuals, however, just as America did after the war. My brother considered it a *mitzwe* (good deed) to be interned in Switzerland. He had all of the freedoms except walking outside by himself. He wrote of his experiences in his book, *Swiss Diary of an Interned Person*. He once confided in me that he would not have regretted it to be interned like that for his entire life. He reached the ripe age of one hundred with the exception of nineteen days, which would have made it a long, long time.

My brother, Hans, who lived in Holland with our mother, worked for the underground, which, by the way, was willing to spirit him to England. He refused. He would not let our old mother live by herself. They both died in the concentration camps.

The most famous member of our family is Louis Lewandowski. He was a composer of liturgical music which is still played all over the world and there is a seventy-minute tape in existance which plays forty of his compositions. He was born in 1821 and died in 1894. When he was twelve years old, his mother died. He was a soloist in a boy choir. Music was his life. In 1844, Louis was invited by the Berlin Academy to be Choir Director at Oranienburgerstrasse Temple. A street in Tel Aviv was later to be named Louis Lewandowski Street. At the commemoration of the one hundredth year of his death, East Germany issued two stamps: one showing the synagogue where he officiated and the other bearing his likeness...unbelievable, yet true that Germany did this to honor a Jew.

Louis had two children, a son and a daughter: Dr. Abraham A. Lewandowski, it was reported, was acquainted with Albert

In 1994, East Germany issued two stamps in honor of
Louis Lewandowski on the 100th anniversary of his death.

Photograph of Synagogue Oranienburgerstrasse in Berlin,
the temple where Louis Lewandowski officiated for many years.
Courtesy of Siegbert Wollstein

Einstein; Miriam (Martha) Lewandowski married the famous philosopher, Hermann Cohen (1842-1918), who taught in Marburg, Germany. In later years, Professor Cohen's eyesight failed him and Miriam was the person who recorded his thoughts, thus preserving them for all time. Far into the future, Professor Wasserstrom of Reed College in Portland, Oregon, conducted a seminar on Professor Cohen in the spring of 1998. Sadly, we do know that Miriam was deported to Theresienstadt, where she was murdered in 1942.

One of the twelve children of Hermann Lewandowski was Isidor, a chason at one of the synagogues in Hamburg where the Lewandowski family was more or less concentrated. Uncle Isidor had a son, Manfred, who became a famous chason at the Friedenstemple in Berlin. When Hitler became Chancellor of Germany, Manfred fled to Paris where he lived for a few years. The interesting thing is that he was willing to take the two children of my brother, Herbert, to the United States, but their parents refused to let them go (the uncircumcised boy and his young sister). He himself settled in Philadelphia where he obtained a cantorial position and lived there for many years.

Reflections

Ever so often one has to draw a line, like an accountant, and figure one's net-worth, not necessarily in dollars and cents but in spiritual value. What did I set out to do? What are my ambitions? Am I getting there?

Having been brought up in the post-war period of the First World War in Germany by parents broken from the devaluation of the mark, I vowed that I should do better. I see my worried father and my tired mother in front of my mental eye and it was they who instilled me with the desire to work hard, disciplining myself to a work day free of hourly borderlines.

On the spiritual side, I felt that I could contribute to the betterment of the world. Being young, one is optimistic in spite of my experiences even then with the unfair distribution of rights and privileges. Already in school in the 1920s, I felt the daily growing of anti-Semitism, the build-up of hate, with which nearly every Arian prided himself.

War to me has always been the most abominable expression between human beings, hate for the sake of hate, and yet I realized early that a pacifist is a man who loves freedom to the point where he feels compelled to fight for it.

I adore the golden middle of the road. I believe in give and take, in arbitration. The only animal which fights its own species is the human animal. Every war has been fought to wipe out all future wars – and yet they occur with regularity. Labor fights management; Whites fight Blacks; Protestants fight Catholics. Unfortunately, the list of adversaries is endless.

There were two factions of youth, Jewish youth, in my home town: those who felt safe and strong in their German heritage and the others who felt that Israel (at that time, Palestine) was the only solution. Even here, within the same religion, these factions did not understand each other. When we had group discussions, I was chosen as a go-between; seemingly I was the only non-radical.

Come to think of it, I was really never young. I had to work hard to make my grades in school and thus never developed an interest in sports. I left school when I was sixteen years old and started working. My father apprenticed me in the China and Housewares section of a department store and in the short span of six years I advanced to the position of a buyer.

In August, 1933, I was fired since management could not permit itself to show my Jewish face to its clientele. I crossed the border to Holland where my older brother had gone seven years earlier. He lived in Utrecht and I moved to Amsterdam. I became a peddler of groceries, selling mostly to other German refuges who had sought a life elsewhere. In 1935, I married the girl I had left behind and we struggled together instead of separately. Hitler's hordes grew by leaps and bounds and soon we realized that there was no security from him, even in a foreign land; Holland, after all, bordered on Germany. We emigrated to the United States in 1937 where I started out again at exactly the same point as I had ten years earlier, as a stockboy in a department store.

Realizing the utter ignorance under which even the U.S.A. labored at that time in regards to the danger from Hitler, I tried to so some missionary work and became the editor of the local immigrant paper. My outcries were interpreted as "warmongering." Oh, what I would have given at that time to become a member of the State Department, teaching the diplomats the rudiments of diplomacy! Naturally, this was only a dream, since I did not have the education for it. Another German-Jewish boy, better equipped, must have had the same dream and found it fulfilled. The boy was Henry Kissinger. It is my opinion that he did an excellent job.

Spiritual assets: without them, life would be equal to the existance of a cow in the pasture. Spirit is to life what love is to sex. Only a person who brings joy to living can enjoy life. Enjoying also means participating, contributing, giving back. Since it is impossible to help all the needy causes, I help those close to my heart. I believe in Israel. I believe in the Democratic Party and in Common Cause, which is the political watchdog. I believe in writing, whenever the spirit moves me, and that seems to be my drummer.

Israel not only needs us, we need Israel. Let us never forget 1938 when the doors of refuge hermetically closed. I repeat, let us *never* forget it, because there are no guarantees that those open doors are not needed again.

I believe in friendship, in doing good, if possible anonymously. Fortune has been with us; my wife and I are comparatively healthy and financially comfortable. The vow I made as a child, I put to reality. I only wish that I could have helped my parents to an easier life. Since one cannot go back but only forward, I try to help those close to me to ease their travel on the road of life.

Friendship and understanding are life's greatest personal awards, thus giving living its richest contents.

What is my spiritual testament? To be what I am! I try to express myself, yet have consideration for the other fellow's needs. I wish that the world could be taught to do away with hate and greed and that we could eliminate poverty through better education for all. Education should not be the responsibility of the local school system and the availability of tax money, but guaranteed to all as a matter of constitutional right. The problem is not integration or segregation; it is education. Give a child a chance according to his mental capabilites. A child who dislikes book-learning is usually well equipped with his hands. Teach him or her a trade but also, always, the principals of ethics, of living in a society which one has to respect if we want that society to respect us. Personally, I believe that we are too permissive. No matter how seriously a person batters the foundation of our society, we forgive and forget. Were the punishment to fit the crime, crime would outlaw itself because it would become a losing proposition. Punishment, therefore, must be severe.

People are as varied as the flowers in the field. I like to listen to other people's ambitions. I enjoy reading biographies about great men who struggled to make this world a better place to live in even though they knew, as I know, that their trojan effort added just an iota of betterment to the boiling pot of humanity.

What are my contributions? Words, words and more words.

Revisiting the Past

Opus 1970: First European Trip

Somehow it felt right, after a very smooth plane ride to London, to find ourselves on a boat crossing the English Channel to Hoek van Holland since thirty-three years earlier we had crossed that same channel in the opposite direction. We had left Europe in search of a new home, America, having only a very foggy notion of what the future would bring. Now we were coming back to the Continent for a visit (this time, first class) to revive memories, many with sad undertones. Yet, we felt that the trip would do us good. We had left the Continent fleeing from the terrible Hun. We came back as Americans, well established and so very happy with our adopted home that we found ourselves feeling like strangers, even in Germany, that country which once we called home.

Walking the streets of Amsterdam, which we remembered as the city with just one skyscraper, we now saw many dotting the otherwise charming landscape. A new spirit had taken hold of the people, a general feeling of brotherhood even with the Germans, who, not too long ago, had destroyed their cities and the hundreds of thousands of people living in them. How was this possible? Every twenty five years, a new generation grows up with memories which do not include the events with which their parents are burdened. This should explain to some extent the course history is taking in our own country where youth has an entirely different concept of duty and responsibility from that of their parents. People only know what they see and hear on the television screen; Western culture hears one side of the story and the Eastern Block another. People travel nearly exclusively in their own circles. Basically, the world is divided into two ideologies, democracy and dictatorship, ideas which can never merge. It seems inevitable that eventually we will die together, the only togetherness the human race is able to produce. Though memories are short as a whole, hate lives on.

From our hotel room in Amsterdam, we looked over the roofs nearby and spotted one building labeled with the year it was built: 1740. I wondered how often this piece of real estate had been written off in two hundred and thirty years, how many owners it has had and how the building itself must feel about the changes outside on the street it has been witness to for so long.

The Rijks Museum is a must for everyone visiting Holland. Going there on a Sunday afternoon, we were to meet crowds of people racing through it, hippies and yippies, who probably sought shelter from the rain outside since on Sundays there is no entrance fee. If the Old Masters knew that all they could expect from the public was a quick glance, they would have been discouraged to have spent hours and hours painting, adding a stroke here and there for emphasis, when now people don't even stop to look.

No journey could have been more appropriate than a visit to the house where we had lived for two years. Only after we saw the stone steps leading up to the apartment did we realize that this indeed was the right place. Children who played outside wanted to get into the picture we took, little realizing that history would disassociate itself from them, children whose grandparents were probably born around the time that we lived there. Then, a wide open field faced our apartment; now, no more; endless rows of houses have gobbled up that gaping beautiful emptiness.

Wherever you look there are people, human beings who do not look any different from us. That is another fluke of human fraility, that we are able to hate others so deeply when actually we are so alike. We all have the same ambitions, similar desires, the wish to express ourselves, to crow at least once before night falls. What a coming and going! We indeed consider it a privilege to come, once again, before we go.

We just passed the city of Utrecht on the train, a university town where my brother lived in the twenties and thirties and from where he fled to France, then to Switzerland. The Dome winked at us as if to say, "I remember when you walked beneath me, around me, oh, so long ago with your brother and his family, then consisting of parents and two very small children. The Nazis came and the Nazis went. I am still here." Those children, hopefully, must be adults somewhere.

In the aisle of the overcrowded train, two young people are sitting on their luggage. Their visible possession seems to be their hair and a comb to go with it. They are very much "in sex," one can see. The girl is attractive, still young and she smokes one cigarette after the other. I can visualize her not too many years from now when her beauty is gone, emphysema takes her place (beauty must be feminine) and sex (who is he?) walks out the door. When emphysema (what an attractive name for such a ugly sickness) becomes this young man's wife, then comes the real test.

We are in Germany now. The question comes up of how to act. Should we be the American who comes over expecting to be understood with his English language (Why speak German? Let them learn English!) or switch the memory bank back? I am tempted to do just that, be a clown, act more German than the Germans do, maybe join into the chorus about "the damn yankee," just for the heck of it. A close friend of mine once said, "Paul, for the life of me, I cannot imagine your getting mad ever," and frankly I agree. Why? Does getting upset change anything really? No. Therefore, not getting upset certainly does not change a thing either. The result is the same. They have their ulcers and I my equilibrium. What does hate produce? Nothing of value. How can we ever have peace if we do not start to build understanding? Just as an example, were the Arabs not so blinded to hate Israel and vice versa, Israelis could go into the Arab lands as friends to help them irrigate the desert, of which there is an abundance. In spite of govermental propaganda, Arab and Jew as a people would like to live in peace and prosperity.

There is the Kaufhof in Koblenz, the place where I worked as the youngest buyer in the organization, then called by the name of Leonard Tietz. Since the building had a new front, it indicated to me that it must have been bombed out by the Allies. (Now, now, Paul, practice what you preach! No joyful feelings, please.)

Soon the train will take us to Wiesbaden, where we will leave it. This is my wife's birthplace. Therefore, it will have a flavor all of its own, which I am trying to bring back to my palate. Here it was that I worked as an Assistant Buyer preceding my stay in Koblenz and here in Wiesbaden it was that I met my wife. How could we resist revisiting the very house where she lived with her parents and where I courted her? Looking at the directory of the tenants, lo and behold, we spotted the name of a family who had lived there thirty-four years ago! Needless to say, we rang the doorbell and a gentleman opened the door. For the very first time in my life, I saw my wife speechless with emotion and I had to jump into the breech. After giving this fine old gentleman a bit of a refresher course, he recognized "his Edith." A real con-fab was had and a liqueur raised in a toast, hoping that we would meet again. It was he who had bought some of the furni-ture from her parents when they left Germany and we had another memory-filled look at it. Going down the same stairs which I used to race up to pick up my date (three floors!), I could not resist stopping at the foot of them and kissing her with the same fervor (I hoped).

We stayed at the Schwarze Bock, a hotel at which we used to look from the outside only with a certain amount of envy because it was here where the rich Americans used to stay when they came for the cure. Little did we dream then that someday we would be one of the guests to stay here. Naturally, we would not pass up that chance even had we to pay twice the price. What quiet refined comfort, sleeping under feather quilts.

The next day, we bought some authentic "Rucksaecke" (knapsacks) for our two small grandsons, whose parents are real outdoor-type people.

Speaking of culture, we had some excellent cake in a "Konditorei" and later attended the opera. And so the days of wine and roses passed.

On our itinerary it says, "Catch train to Lucerne, Switzer-land." We planned it that way so that we could see some of the beauty of the Rhineland on our way. Later we discovered that the famous Rhineland which we remembered as being so green and the Rhine as so blue, seemed barren and the Rhine so grey. Only the old castles livened the scenery and fired the imagination. It is so easy to fly over everything in a plane, above the clouds, seeing the blue sky but no earth. Traveling along in this traditional manner, we also realized how very small the distances are between one town and another. Wiesbaden-Mainz, which is a five-minute train ride, used to be considered quite a journey in our young days. We were in Mainz only two or three times then because it was simply too far away. The vastness of America has created an entirely different impression in our minds. Germany was never big; now it has become even smaller through the division that took place in 1945.

As everywhere, the people with money are living it up. The industrialists in Germany travel all over the world, have the hourly wage earners do their work for them and members of the Third World come on temporary visas to do the menial jobs.

The weather was rather cold for April when we arrived in Lucerne. Snow was on the rooftops and shiver was in our bodies. We went up Mt. Pilatus by chairlift, a beautiful ascent with a view of Lucerne and the Vierwaldstaetter See, looking back and seeing part of the mountain looking up, up and up. We were fortunate that the sun was shining at that moment, enabling us to take a few pictures. The further up we got, the foggier the notion became that we could actually see Mt. Pilatus close by. All we really saw up there was the restaurant sticking out of the snow. What we were able to do was to have a marvelous body-warming European-sized plate of soup which we ate cozily with European-sized soup spoons; (in America we would call them tablespoons). They know how to make good soup everywhere in Europe and how to serve it so you can enjoy it with gusto along with the feeling of having warmed the heart, the stomach, the hands and those cold feet.

Going down, it snowed, snowed and snowed some more and we fled as quickly as possible to snuggle under the feather covers of our hotel beds where we took an afternoon snooze in lieu of investigating the sights of the city further. After all, we were on vacation, summer vacation supposedly, so that we could do what we pleased and we were pleased to do what we could; namely, sleep.

Tonight we will go to the Stadttheater to hear a Schauspiel and it will be then that we benefit from the rest taken, listening with open and wide-awake ears to the German language play. German, by now, has returned to our tongue and rolls off with the ease of the R's that are so much a part of it. The play is "Weh Dem Der Luegt" ("Woe To Him Who Lies") by Franz Grillparzer.

The play was a rare experience. We went back to the hotel and wondered how good it felt that a modern people can still attend and enjoy these old wisdoms. Grillparzer is somewhat like a German Shakespeare, conveying old but true thoughts in stilted fashion. He was born in 1791 in Vienna and was most unsuccessful during his lifetime, finding recognition only after his death at the age of ninety-one.

As it turned out, we experienced a very special treat. The night we attended was the premiere of the play in Lucerne and one of the main roles was played by Mr. Arnold Putz, who not only celebrated his seventieth birthday, but also his fiftieth year as an actor. After the performance, a celebration took place right on the stage with the curtain open, honoring Mr. Putz in front of the full house. Many patrons handed him gifts and voiced tributes.

Speaking of rare instances, one comes to my mind: Many years ago when I attended the famous horseraces in the Bois de Boulogne near Paris, the public did not agree with the decision of the judge and as an addendum hailed stones from all directions at the poor decision-maker "protected" in a glass house in the middle of the field. He finally decided to lie flat on the floor to protect himself from the hail storm. The Chief of Police had to speak over the loud-speaker system, then already invented, to quiet the enraged elite. Can you imagine Parisiens attired in their formal black suits and grey top hats acting like that?

Now we are on the train from Lucerne to Geneva, via Bern. Though snow still covers the landscape, here and there we see the green of the meadows, the rugged hills, the solidly-built houses with everything clean and peaceful. Even when we read the newspapers, there seem to be few problems in Switzerland; they are all somewhere else in the world.

When my brother fought for the Germans in the First World War, he pleaded with my father to uproot himself and move his family to peaceful Switzerland. My father did not listen because he was not only settled, but also set in his ways. It was a serious mistake he made because later in the German inflation, he lost everything he had worked for all his life. My mother and twin brother would not have been caught in the onslaught upon their very lives by Hitler had he listened.

We arrived at the Geneva train station punctually. The electric train service is clean and efficient and should serve as an example to American transportation systems.

My brother, Herbert, and his family were there to greet us. They took us to our hotel near their apartment, where we freshened up. Later, we joined them in their home. It was so nice to be with my brother again, to see how he lives, to know where he works on his books and to get to know each other after so many turbulent years, to exchange brotherly feelings, to learn of incidents about which I did not know and all the little things that tie a family together.

Living space is at a premium in Switzerland. Only the ultra-rich can afford to own a home. Everybody else lives in an apartment and is happy to find one, since even apartments are rare.

I saw my brother's den where he works. Books decorate three of the four walls. Many of the books are written by himself and others, including autographed editions from contemporary writers together with handwritten letters sent to him by authors from many parts of the world. His hobby of collecting over a lifetime necessitates the donation of timeless papers to the local museum. As readers may know, be they writers, composers or painters, very few find popularity during their lifetime. Vincent van Gogh did not sell one painting while he was alive and had it not been for the generosity of his brother, Theo, he would have died of hunger. Today his paintings sell for many millions of dollars each.

I had intended to ask my brother some "brotherly questions"

about his life, but somehow one does not get around to bringing such pertinent subjects to the fore. Was your life truly a happy one? Do you feel that it was a worthwhile one? Did you do the things you set out to do? One thing I do know: he always wanted to be a writer in spite of terrible interruptions, persecution and having been forced to flee from the hordes of Hitler, not once, not twice, but three times. He was separated from his family for years before being reunited – and yet he remained an idealist.

Geneva is the seat of the United Nations in Europe. It is difficult to ascertain what this organization actually has accomplished. One thing is for sure: it has become a behemoth with many buildings and thousands of employees which make a living from it, pretending to bring about peace. Everything in this world in the final analysis becomes self-consuming. War is still very much with us.

Breaking bread with my brother and his large family was symbolic of the closeness of our family ties. We were their guests at a fine restaurant where we ate in style; two wines were served with dinner in addition to the seltzers, which is standard equipment. Being together tied some of the loose ends, drinking together loosened the tight knots, talking about many problems, unsolvable as life itself, brought about harmony and a sense of belonging. Granted, our lives and scopes are different, he being an intellectual and I just a cool businessman. When rising from the table each one of us is dutybound to pick up his parcel, even though he might be inclined to leave it there or at least some of its contents for the waiter to pick up with the bread crumbs. Often problems seem to be unsolvable, similar to the language problem which befell this small family unit, some speaking French only, some French and German and none English. To unite the world, first of all we must have a world language. Somehow, the mere fact that people can understand one another creates a pacifying atmosphere. When you speak the same language, you feel akin.

Switzerland is an anachronism. To be neutral and headquarters of the International Red Cross is fine, but at the same time, through lenient banking laws, Switzerland destroys world conscience and decency. To permit every criminal of high finance to find a safe place for his ill-begotten money in a Swiss bank has devilish undertones. In other words, Switzerland puts herself outside the decency of a world community in the selfish interest of financial gain. Switzerland giving a home to the United Nations is comparable to the humanitarianism of a Carnegie, who built libraries after exploiting his workers mercilessly.

We are in Milano now, which was once called Mailand when it still belonged to the Austrian Empire. They have indeed worked successfully to transform this city into an American-type metropolis. Skyscrapers now ruin the skyline of that beautiful old city where cathedrals once reigned. Opera lovers that we are, our first step was in the direction of the world's most famous opera house, La Scala, where "La Callas" made her name and fame. Looking at the house inside from the direction of the stage, one sees a beautiful baroque-type theatre; however, looking from the theatre towards the stage, which after all is a bit more important, one sees many seats behind the columns which obstruct the vision from the only available seats on the balconies. Good first-floor seats belong to the Milanese who have season tickets. Furthermore, we heard a second-class Rigoletto which only added to the disappointment. Even though the Portland Opera has not the same world renown, a better Rigoletto was heard from its stage. When Guilda in Milano befuddled herself, you could hear the public's reaction from the gallery down; at the end of the act, she did not have the courage to come out in front of the curtain since boos certainly would have been her just reward.

The point of greatest interest was Venice. There is a saying, "See Venice and die." I would not go that far. Leaving the railroad station, we took a *vaporetto,* a motorized boat which is the equivalent of a taxi. Now you will understand the saying, "He missed the boat." Venice is a very old city built around canals. Seeing that a jail was located next to a palazzo with just a little bridge between the two put my imagination to work. Let us say that you insulted the host by not praising his or her culinary art; they could just open a door and push you out into the canal – never to be seen or heard from again.

The main attraction is the Piazza San Marco, impressive by its very magnificence. We had a hotel room right behind the square, very charming and picturesque. What we would call a street was a small alley where I could observe the continuous foot-traffic from the large window of our room. Happy young lads whistling while going to work often had a song upon their lips as well. As you probably know from their American counterparts, Italians are a cheerful, jolly people. I remember seeing a little boy of about six years of age wearing dark-framed glasses, his leather satchel worn on his back (as all kids do in Europe), studiously walking along; to me, he was the miniature of a future college professor. The proverbial beauty of Italian girls was not in evidence at all. Can it be that the Italian mothers kept their daughters at home, knowing that I was in town? Venice, a city geared to a multitude of visitors, has shops everywhere. Everybody lives upstairs, some up and up.

We elevatored up the Companile, located right in front of the Duomo, from where we had a magnificent view over all of Venice. From there we saw the many islands, the multitude of churches as well as the quaintness of hundreds of red-tiled roofs. No skyscrapers yet to mar this beautiful fairytale city. Looking from above or walking through the streets, one feels transformed into an age long gone by. Had some of the old Venecians been frozen for a thousand years and then awakened by a thaw, they would not know that time had progressed.

A trip to Venice is not complete without visiting one of the many islands. The most famous and best known to me is Murano, where the renowned glass by the same name is manufactured. To tour the gloryhole, as the opening of the glass furnace is called, is free, but not the finished product. There a very eager salesman tries to sell his products from a very elaborate showroom.

I am sure that only a select group of travelers visit the Jewish Quarter of the city. The name *ghetto* comes from here and has become part of many languages. The synagogue was closed; however, a poor Jew was standing in the entrance doorway to parcel out a bit of information in three languages. He himself was a remnant from one of the East European countries, a refugee who had lost his entire family in the Holocaust. Speaking to him, I realized how the moss of time gradually covers up everything; still there are deep craters which affliction has left behind. This poor man drags his burden with even more tenacity than we.

We heard an opera by Rossini – Armide – never before played in Venice, or, for that matter, anywhere else. Someone removed it from the dust of time and we discovered it to be a charming opera. The Venice Opera House may not be so well known as La Scala in Milano, but it proved able to present a better performance.

Now we are traveling along the Mediteranean to Nice, which affords us a dazzling sight of different proportions as the grandeur of modern buildings, palatial hotels and meticulously kept gardens come into view. This coast, brightly lit by a sun set into a clear sky, invites the elegant living for which the Riviera is famous. Suddenly one wishes to be ten years older, retired, living and enjoying, being here forever, not to have to return, grinding out some more of that *moneta* to afford this type of living. All you do here is nothing, particularly when you can look at hand-knitted bikinis. It is quite a test to keep your knit-wits about you.

Castles are as plentiful as they are along the Rhine in Germany. Little did these potentates of old know how much they would one day contribute to the tourist trade in the twentieth century by building these fortresses. Castle builders of a more modern type are the wealthy industrial barons who, at the turn of the century, started to build their villas on the Riviera and instinctively picked the most beautiful spots.

Monaco is a storybook tale, which is real – the best description I can give that principality. Here Prince Ranier was able to charm Grace Kelly into becoming a real princess. Too bad that this reality was only short-lived. At noon, the guard changes along with the office and domestic help, this through the backdoor with a great deal less fanfare than in front.

29

Revisiting the past also includes somber moments. I visited the grave of my father in Kassel-Bettenhausen, Germany, where he is buried at the Jewish Cemetary. He died a natural death in January, 1936, only three months after he attended our wedding in Amsterdam. A commemorative plaque also gives homage to my mother and twin brother, who died in the Holocaust.

Now we are in Paris, the city of famous museums: the Louvre, where all of the Old Masters are assembled; the Musee Jeu de Pomme, where the younger masters of the nineteenth century found a home: Monets, Manets, Van Goghs, Gauguins, Matisses, Renoirs, Lautrecs. My favorite museum in Paris, however, is the Rodin Museum, which I visited for the first time about forty years ago. I feel very deeply about Rodin's interpretation of human emotion. "Breathing marble," I would call his work.

Rather than being repetitious about the many sights in Paris, I like to mention monuments less talked about. There are two memorials in the shadow of Notre Dame commemorating the victims of the Nazi occupation. Many building still show the bullet holes where Jews and other hapless people were murdered in cold blood.

You may recall that the city from which we started our memory trip was London. Now we planned to spend some time there. Needless to say, we visited the British Museum with its Portland Vase, the Rosetta Stone and many other rare tidbits. Personally I was fascinated with the assemblage of letters, the collection of autographs being my particular hobby. I soon realized how puny my own collection is, but then I did not have the help of kings and queens. One consolation I did have was that many of the famous handwritings resemble mine in illegibility.

Some time was spent at Westminister, where I stepped right on top of the plaque commemorating Winston Churchill to whom I wrote years earlier requesting an autograph. His secretary advised me that Mr. Churchill was not in the habit of doing that. (Now I own an autograph from the secretary.) You see what happens to famous people who shun autograph collectors? There are many world-renowned people buried there. As the guide quipped so well, "I would rather be stepped upon than forgotten." (Which most of us will be.)

Nowhere did we find the fear that is with us in the United States which is to be mugged when you are alone on the street at night. That which we falsely call freedom will become our undoing unless it is checked by firm action from the still silent majority. Freedom accompanied by fear has no value. Crime, rioting and drug addiction are a form of sickness, a cancer on the society which, if not removed, will infest its deadliness upon all of us. Naziism, a similar form of sickness, had to be rooted out with the sword. Democracy has come to mean a permissive society, which is very tragic.

We are back home visiting the present. In spite of all the shortcomings we notice here in America, we certainly would not want to live anywhere else. We are not only back home, but we feel at home, actually for the first time in our lives.

The Yanks Are Coming

After a thirty-year absence from the East Coast, it was quite a revelation to visit the cradle of American history, Washington D.C. What a font of information is gathered there. What an architectural beauty in the marble palaces and monuments. What a feeling of magnificence to see the overpowering majesty of the Capitol building, the sense of security which the Supreme Court exhumes, the wisdom that is gathered in the Library of Congress and the aesthetic wealth which is represented in the National Museum of Modern Art.

Granted, the West has San Francisco, but it is somewhat like the relationship between the solemnity of a grandfather and his youthful grandchild.

The structure of the family is the binding thread between the peoples of this earth. It was Aunt Martha Lavender from Pittsburgh, Pennsylvania, whose compassion made it possible to bring many members of our family out of the mire of Germany to the Land of Opportunity, America. Little did Uncle Max know, being long deceased and the first member of the family to come to the United States in the 1880's, that his emigration would be such a prophetic step. Their children, particularly Jerry, a dermatologist, and his sister, Hilda, shared in this task. It was Hilda whom I visited on my way to Washington, an eighty-seven-year-old youngster whose mental alertness is as keen today as on the day I left Pittsburgh so many years ago. We have always felt a certain strong bond although we expressed it only in an occasional exchange of letters, hers always adorned with dried flowers, somehow her trademark. Seeing her again reminded me of a weathered leather flask, holding a delicious seasoned wine. One says that the interest of our investment are our children. I met with one of Hilda's two sons, Lee, and his charming wife, Nesha, sparkling with intellect and reflecting the wealth of love her husband must be heaping upon her.

One of the blessed immigrants is Lotte, whom I remembered so well announcing the birth of her baby, aptly named Paul.

I met this young man, now in his thirties. It was gratifying to learn that there is great interest in the background of the family Lavender-Lewandowski.

Many years ago, my mother had assembled a family tree which I have kept up-to-date. It is a good feeling to know that Judaism is still practiced and that the young generation is proceeding to help newcomers. More Russian refugees are now entering the United States. Yet it is tragic that all these people know is that the Communist government has them typed as "Jew" in their official papers, yet that is the first and the last thing that they know about Judaism. They have never been in a synagogue, nor have they seen a Torah or any other Jewish religious object. They are Jews – that is all. Wherever they go, they not only have to learn a new language, they also have to acquaint themselves with a new heritage. Let us never forget that this is the Russian way of freedom.

We continued our family visits in Washington D.C. One afternoon was spent with our cousin, Helen Diamond, in her comfortable apartment in the Northwest district of this lively town, not far from Embassy Row. After so many years, it was an emotional meeting, exchanging family news, which may have escaped in the dearth of correspondence. Fate did not deal the best of cards to her, yet she always solved her problems with strength and fortitude, assets for which I always admired her. The name, Diamond, entered our family when my grandfather on my father's side fell in love with Jenny Diamond in 1848. It was interesting for me to hear from that side of the family the information which is not part of the aforementioned family tree.

City of Washington...here we are! Our first trip was to the Library of Congress, which found my wife's unreserved favor. Books are one of her hobbies and this library is one of the wonders of our civilization. One of the Gutenberg Bibles is on display along with an eighth century Hebrew manuscript. It was a joy beyond compare to find most of my brother's books, Dr. Herbert Lewandowski, written in German, catalogued there. Also a book written by my brother-in-law, Dr. Frank Rosenthal, entitled *The Jews of Des Moines.*

Just to visit a tiny part of the wealth of information that is gathered here, one has to have the stamina of an Olympic runner. A great help is the "tour mobile" which deposits you and picks you up at all points of interest. The Smithsonian alone compromises ten different museums and, it is said, were you to view each object for just a minute, it would take a hundred years to see it all. One of the most frequented museums is the Air and Space Museum where among the multitude of objects you will find the first Wright Brothers airplane along with the space capsule which carried our astronauts to the moon. To tell us more about this and other ventures, two excellent movies are shown.

The new East Wing of the Natural Art Museum displays most prominently a huge Calder mobile while the Hirschhorn Museum has an excellent collection of sculpture. As an admirer of Rodin's art, I was happy to see pieces I had not seen in the Rodin Museum in Paris. Where does one begin to report and where does one end? Actually there is neither a beginning nor an ending. One jumps right in...and wanders and wonders.

Since government and people are interrelated, I intentionally brought some of my family history into this report.

My family has some fame since Louis Lewandowski, the composer of Jewish music, was the brother of my grandfather and his daughter married the famous philosopher, Hermann Cohen, who taught in Marburg, Germany, and is often quoted with Kant and Schlegel. Dr. Cohen numbered among his many students the famous Russian writer, Boris Pasternak, author of *Dr. Zhivago.*

The National Gallery of Art has the most fabulous collection of modern paintings. Monet, Manet, Cezanne and foremost in my wife's eyes, Alfred Sisley. She fell in love with his style when we visited the Jeaux de Pomme in Paris several years ago. If ever a Sisley should be missing, I suggest to start the investigation at our home.

The National Museum of History and Technology featured an Einstein exhibit. Among many other documents, I was thrilled by the exchange of letters between Einstein and Siegmund

Freud in German as I was able to read and understand each and every word. It may not generally be known that Einstein was a great pacifist but, as always, marching boots will trample any such ideologies. Besides its fabulous collection of diamonds, the museum also has a fine assortment of crystal and fine china from all over the world. I knew that once there was a china factory in the town of my birth, Kassel (Hessen), Germany, but it took my visit to Washington D.C. to see a sample of that era.

I should not forget to mention the Botanical Gardens, where eight thousand kinds of exotic flowers, fruits and other plants are displayed.

It was a sunny day when we traveled to Williamsburg by bus. Our driver was a former history professor turned bus driver, since the latter profession is much more lucrative. We certainly benefitted by his explanations which were so vivid that we could well imagine a Colonial army coming out of the woods on the left side of the road almost any moment. It was the Rockefeller (quite a feller) Foundation which financed the reconstruction of this beautiful colonial town. Before 1776, it was the nation's capital for sixty years. The highlight is the Governor's Palace with its brick facade and beautiful wrought iron gates. We visited some of the residences and learned that the kitchens were separated from the house to protect the mansions from the danger of fire.

I doubt that there was as much commercialism in Williamsburg then as there is now. Leather and silver displayed for sale, maybe yes. Now you may find Wedgwood from England, Leerdam from Holland and Stieff with his reproductions. Lots of taverns could be seen. They played a great role in those days since they were the only gathering places next to a visit to the church. There was no telephone, record-playing machine, radio or television to keep the people home.

One cannot help but be intrigued by the sense of history which surrounds one: Fredricksburg, Richmond, Jamestown, Yorktown and others paint several-hundred-year-old pictures before the mental eye. How lucky we are that we did not have to wear battle uniforms and muskets. We owe our forefathers a debt of gratitude. Arlington Cemetary bears witness to heroism through the ages. A week before John F. Kennedy was assassinated, he visited there and, looking down from the Lee Mansion, he was heard to have said, "I could stay here forever." The eternal light is also part of Jewish tradition and the burning flame at the graveside should remind every one of us that a spirit, once kindled, will live on forever.

Standing at the Jefferson Memorial and looking toward the Washington Obelisk mirrored in the reflecting pool as is the White House beyond, I can only compare this view to Paris and the Champs Elysee. No wonder the Frenchman L'Enfant envisioned it. One of the most awe-inspiring monuments in the world is the Lincoln Memorial.

The John F. Kennedy Center for the Performing Arts differs from the other memorials in that it is a center for the living. The grand foyer measures 630 feet with nary a bench to rest your weary bones upon. Yet, there is a bust of John F. to cheer you up and a row of crystal chandeliers hanging from the high ceiling to direct your glances upward. Three theatres form the Art Center and there is a built-in white marble wall with some of John F. Kennedy's sayings chiselled into the stone on the Potomac side. The Eisenhower Theatre is mainly for stage plays, the Opera House (you guessed it) for opera and ballet and the Concert Hall for symphonies and other musical presentations. All of the appointments are gifts from other countries: two stone murals from Germany, a fabulous Waterford chandelier from Ireland, and from Mexico, two colorful paintings entitled, "Poem to Fire," decorate the walls of the Eisenhower Theatre. Another chandelier, a gift from Austria, adorns the ceiling of the Opera House. Israel's gift fills the north lounge of the Concert Hall: the ceiling is painted in the most lively of colors with one center wall covered with a metal sculpture based on Psalm 150, depicting Judaism from the times of the Bible to the present day.

We attended a performance in the Concert Hall of the National Symphony Orchestra under the baton of the former Russian cellist, Mstislav Rostropovich. At another time, Itzhak Perlman played the violin for Mendelssohn's "Violin Concerto."

Here is proof of mind over body, since this young Israeli contacted polio early in his youth and did not let this interfere with his ambition.

We saw government in action at the Supreme Court which happened to be hearing the case of "The State of Washington versus an Indian Tribe." Apparently the tribe had abused privileges given it under previous legislation. Unfortunately, the Congress and the Senate both were so overcrowded with visitors that we preferred not to stand in line.

To add a bit of humor, there was one line we could not avoid, the food line, and while we were waiting, we overheard the man in front determining that the two families ahead of him were the Browns and the Blacks; his name was White. When I added that our name was Lavender, he accepted this with disbelief. What this proves is that we do indeed live in a colorful world.

We cannot leave Washington D.C. without paying homage to the Metro System which is Washington's subway. It works efficiently and it is very easy to find one's way about. The city is working hard on expanding the system.

"The Yanks" are returning home to the West, bringing with them a renewed hope that the country will survive.

Part II
Family

My Very Young Daughter's Personal Prayer

I pray for Mommy, Daddy, Eleonore, Grandpa and Grandma, Aunt Ruth, Uncle Frank, Elden and Ilene. I pray for their dog and cat, our former cat, Chomo Lungma, and I pray for our present cat, Jupiter Sputnik, a little more because he is not well. I pray for the sun, the moon, the stars, the sky, the trees, the ground and the grass. Also I pray for the birds, the bees, the butterflies, for every person, place and thing. I pray for every living person and every non-living person; I pray for every living plant and non-living plant; for every living insect and non-living insect. I pray for every living animal and every non-living animal. I pray for every living thing in the whole world and every non-living thing in the whole world. Last but not least, I pray for You, God, more than anything in the world – and I pray for myself.

A Spell in Paradise

Our first trip to Hawaii was in the year of 1957 when there was only the Royal Hawaiian Hotel and a few smaller hotels to take care of the tourists. It was at that time that the idea of the condominium was born in the Islands. These apartment homes were offered then at the total cost of $5,000.

When the luxury liner, Matsonia, arrived in Honolulu, sailing across the Pacific on her maiden voyage, I was on the dock to receive the maidens of my family who had sailed aboard her. I had flown over and arrived just one hour ahead of them. The activities on the dock could well compare to a three-ring circus, Polynesian style: a military band played as hula girls swayed their hips and gestured with graceful hands; local boys dived for coins thrown from the starboard of the ship and all of the *malahinis,* the new arrivals, wore flower *leis* presented to them by attractive Hawaiian girls.

My flight to the Hawaiian Islands was as smooth as being transported on a flying carpet. The land we reached impressed us like a chapter out of the *Arabian Nights.* Hawaii is a fairyland. Palms gently fan you while you walk in the bright sun as showers, which seem to fall from a gentle sprinkler system, refresh you. The fragrance of plumeria blossoms fills the soft tropical air. The people themselves are a sociologist's dream. A deck of cards could not be better mixed after shuffling. Graceful almond-eyed girls, women with children who show their paternal origin, a sailor from Idaho, a Black from the Gold Coast, all add their characteristics and charm.

The friendliness of these people is beyond description. They are happy-go-lucky people. It seems that what we need on "the mainland" is a tropical sun.

Close friends drove us about the island and played host to us in their home, one of the most beautiful on Pacific Heights, overlooking the ocean and part of the city. Sections of the home are entirely open, forming a unity with the garden. The swimming pool is located on a lower level with the orchid gardens in the back of the house. Chinese lanterns, chest of drawers carved from cherrywood and exquisite pieces of carved ivory are strewn about. Paradise was never like this!

The vacationer's life is a hard one. One is constantly faced with difficult decisions: Shall we stay in the hotel swimming pool or shall we swim in the ocean? Shall we eat once a day or all day long with so many of those tempting tropical fruits staring at you? Cunning as I am, I convinced the family that going shopping would be best at night, thinking that the stores would be closed. As luck would have it, enough of them were open to ruin my scheme. I ended up with a pair of Hawaiian bathing trunks, an aloha shirt and a pair of bermuda shorts. *Muumuus*, sarongs and complete outfits for the ladies of my family followed. What is a *muumuu*? It is a mixture (everything here has to be a mixture!) that lies somewhere between a sack and a nightgown. To me, they look like remnants of a warehouse sale, the clearance stock found in the cellars of missionaries who first came here and covered the beautiful nudity of the Hawaiian people. Had Dior prescribed these fashions, they could not have become more accepted. Every woman looks pregnant in them; fortunately, men are not wearing them yet. How the Hawaiian men seem to love their women chubby. Pound for pound, they must feel that they get more of their honey's worth.

Somehow, it seems to me that the Hawaiians, particularly the young ones, got cheated when they accepted clothing from the Western *haole*, white man. The worst part of the bargain is that now many of the not-so-good-looking whites are running around in a state of dishabille, while the good-looking natives are fully covered.

Did you ever wonder what happens to young hula dancers grown old? They are transferred to the orchestra section to strum the ukulele. Somewhere along the way, they acquire the art of singing, which is part of the job.

The means of making a living are quite varied. Never in my life have I seen so many shoeshine boys and so few shoes to shine. Everybody walks barefoot here, unless he happens to be the doorman of the Royal Hawaiian Hotel. I saw one boy shine somebody's feet. Children start to work at an early age, shining feet, dancing the hula, working in the sugar cane or pineapple fields. Many of the tourists don't realize that Hawaii is more than the sand beach of Waikiki.

We had the good fortune to be in Waikiki on the Fourth of July. The Hawaiians love a good time and fireworks. No law can curb them from expressing their joy. Hundreds of firecrackers and flares were shot off until late into the night, some under the auspices of the hotels, most of them on the initiative of the natives themselves. Soldiers and sailors, in service from the United States, roam around in abundance and add their own special brand of deviltry. Not all of them are as hard boiled as they may appear in their immaculate uniforms. We talked to some of them, nice clean kids, who are homesick rather than roughnecks. A boy just out of school transplanted on an island thousands of miles away from home does not feel so good about it. Often the letters to their family and friends have not been answered because the people back there do not seem to understand that a young man in the Army, Navy or Marines needs that link with home and friends to maintain his mental equilibrium.

Even on an island built for pleasure, business has to be conducted. Pleasure is big business here. As on the mainland, expansion is the secret word of the day. The hotels and vacation facilities grow ever more numerous, made possible by last year's losses.

Somehow I feel that a trip to the Islands could not be complete without probing into their colorful history. The Bishop Museum (the Bishops being one of the "Big Five" families in Hawaii) reveals a wealth of data. These families all were New England missionaries who helped the Polynesians, while profiting themselves. It is fairly certain that the Hawaiians are not of American origin, but rather from Polynesia. Feather capes and ornaments in any form or shape played an important part in the regalia of the royal family. Great Hawaiian names that roll from the tongue like honey carried through their tradition up into the early part of this century.

Religions are manifold. Mormons and Catholics are neck and neck in numerical strength. Race is no handicap in becoming a Mormon. There is also a Jewish congregation in Honolulu. No matter what a person's belief, the religious needs of natives or vacationers can be met.

One Sunday afternoon, we went outrigger riding. Having done nothing all week, I felt that I should have some exercise; thus, I went to work at being "number two man paddle pusher."

Outrigging is a sport in which eight people sit in a canoe-type boat supported by an extra rail held by two crossbars. All eight people paddle hard to get the boat into the surf area, turn the craft toward shore at the right moment under the command of the leader of the boat and paddle mightily to get in front of the wave, only to be caught on your behind to find yourself being propelled towards shore in the same manner as a bar-keeper would expel an unpleasant customer. Speed, which is the foundation of all sports, grips you by the neck and provides the thrills. To get there faster, faster, faster…to where?

One day we went to an authentic Japanese restaurant built in Japanese style, a place where real Japanese food is served by real Japanese to "unreal Japanese" gourmets dressed in kimonos who sit on pillows on the floor. Before them is a low cherrywood table on which many lovely dishes are set, flanked by wooden chopsticks, the Japanese silverware. While the food is prepared in front of your eyes on a charcoal burner, you receive a lesson in the art of handling such chopsticks. When the dinner is finally served, it tastes so different from what you expected that it taxes your brain to decide whether you like it or not. Finally, a green tea is served and perhaps you then join the ranks of those who bemoan the fact that they did not put it to better use as dishwater. Having fully recovered, you can take a walk through the beautiful Japanese gardens which surround the establishment and, if you want to, envy the Japanese beetle who must be living there.

Another of the many highlights of our trip was the visit to the Island of Hawaii proper. A two-engine plane took us there. This was the first flight for the kids who reacted as twentieth-century teenagers do. What is so unusual about this? When do you offer us something really exciting?

At the Hilo airport, a car was waiting for us, a new Chevrolet with all the conveniences of our somewhat older Plymouth at home, with the exception of power steering and power brakes, which we enjoy on our own car. Steering the wheel felt like wrestling with the car every time we made a turn. Luckily I was always on top. The trip to the Volcano House was interspersed with many lava flows, the most interesting being the one of May, 1955. We stood about a foot away from the big hole left by that eruption, steam blowing all around from ventholes nearby. People who live in Hilo, the closest town, told us that they flew over the volcano on that May day, seeing the hot lava spout right under them. Hundreds of cars were approaching the crater, rather than fleeing from it as one might assume. The flow of the lava is comparatively slow and it seems that one can get out of its way easily. Nobody got hurt, even though many houses were lost since the eruption occurred in an area previously unaffected. Eruptions are usually predicted a year ahead of time, but this one crept up on them unannounced.

Arriving at the Volcano House, we took the rim drive which showed us the many lava beds, funnels and blowholes. The road from the Volcano House to Kona is one of the snakiest roads one can encounter. Generally, there is space for only one car; the "other" car is always met in the tightest spot possible, but somehow one passes without fender-bending. Driving continuously for ninety miles and watching for those encounters somehow called to my mind Juliet's query, "Where art thou, Romeo?" We got there finally without being hurt, went to our lanai, a house without windowpanes where screens take the place of glass and bamboo curtains shield us from the sun.

Soon the time came to say farewell to Hawaii proper, the Big Island, the volcano land. They have their troubles too. I heard one volcano say to the other, "Stop blowing your top!"

Back on Oahu, we kept our date with the Navy for a round-trip through Pearl Harbor. This arrangement had been made on the day of our arrival since only a limited number of people can be accommodated every day. Only a few miles from Waikiki Beach, the world's most fantastic playground, you see the other extreme, the burial ground of our Navy, sunk there on December 7, 1941, as Franklin D. Roosevelt so correctly said, "a day of infamy" never to be forgotten.

Today, Pearl Harbor is once more the workshop and storeroom of war machinery. After lengthy discussions in Washington D.C., all the branches of our National Defense – the Army, the Navy, the Air Force and the Marines – were united. The pulse of the entire world is felt here every day. When unrest breaks out in Egypt, part of the fleet starts to move in that direction. The Chief of our Navy launch pointed out to us in no uncertain words the difference between the Pearl Harbor of yesterday and today. Here a taxpayer can witness what his contribution is buying.

Sugarcane and pineapple are the two largest industries of the Islands. Pineapple juice replaces water at the drinking fountains of the Dole Pineapple Cannery, the largest such plant in the world. Most every day, we undertook something special, a new highlight of our trip. A visit to Dole was just that. We saw the machines which remove core, shells and ends from the pineapples at the speed of 105 pineapples per minute. Hundreds of women inspect the fruit, removing imperfections and grading at the same time. To me, a factory of any kind (and I have seen the manufacture of many varied products) is greatly intriguing since it so clearly reveals the ingenuity of the human mind.

My oldest daughter made the acquaintance of a very nice Polynesian-Chinese boy who was charmed with her. On the eve of our departure, he rose at 5:00 AM to gather literally more than a thousand blossoms which he fashioned into a beautiful *lei* with the endless patience that graces these people. To crown it all and to express his feelings for her, he also presented her with an island hat decorated with orchids.

We have had such a wonderful vacation, lasting two weeks, which brought us so much closer together as a family than an average working day is able to do. I also felt a much deeper communication with God and Nature. Being stretched out there in the sun or sitting in the shade of a palm tree without a single pressing care sets one to thinking and evaluating. I felt so grateful for the breath I take, for the health of my family and the spirit which makes it my family, yet for the individuality of each of its members.

M-O-T-H-E-R

M – mistress
O – of
T – the
H – home's
E – edifying
R – rampart

The Problem Solvers
(Written for the benefit of my daughters)

"Meeting, please come to order," rocked Mr. Stool, who chaired at the round-table discussion of the Furniture and Fixture Union at the White House. "This is our monthly get-together," he said, "when we discuss important matters at hand." He continued, saying, "Here, we are masters rather than servants to our fate."

The President was attending a very important meeting at a hotel in Hawaii and the other members of the family were flitting about somewhere.

As always, the Cabinet reminded the conference that anything said here was top-drawer secret.

"Mr. Chairman." With these words, the Lemon Press got the attention of the Table. "We have been very much disappointed about the secrecy with which the goings-on here are treated. We feel that the public is entitled to be informed about everything that is said and heard here. Yes, to the last drop. Even though matters may be sour most of the time. I ask, why should not the people suffer in the same manner as their selected representatives?"

Mr. Bed, from the "Private Chamber," always seemed to have the floor. Since he had known Lincoln and "bedded" every occupant of this famous house, he stood there squarely, his feet very securely on the ground. He reported of the turning and tossing that was going on nightly within his confines. When asked which of his previous guests tossed the most, he said that he would stand on the Fifth Amendment which had been placed in the middle for reasons of insecurity many years ago.

"Order! Order in the house!" bellowed the Gavel and one could see the objects which a busy family had left lying around gather themselves up and return to their proper places. Even the hair, which the First Lady had let down during a recent press conference, picked itself up.

"Mr. Secretary has the Floor," the Chairman acknowledged.

He was a very important man since everything in the nature of address, also of dressing for important occasions, touched his naughty pine. He reminded the gathering of the seriousness that faced everyone in attendance. "Next Saturday night," he said, "there will be an important State Affair and many stuffed shirts are being readied for that occasion."

Mr. Stove, the representative of the Department for the Interior, then entered the heated discussion. He was hot under the "color," being black. He felt that the heat of the debate should not always be centered around him and that someone else should keep the political pot boiling.

The coolest customer attending the gathering was, by all means, Mr. Frigidaire. He suggested that most of the problems facing the country should be put on ice, as the Congress and the Senate have been doing so successfully all along.

Then it was that Mr. Glass spoke up. To him, everything was crystal clear. He spoke out with a beautiful ring in his high-pitched voice and warned about tabling matters that were under advisement. "Everyone should clearly see," he said, "that this would bring about a Crash many times worse than the one in 1929."

How Mr. Knife got to the floor, nobody really knew. As usual, he made his cutting remarks. He said, "I am sick and tired of being separated from my wife, the Fork, by that big fat Dinner Plate, who, in her capitalistic manner, places herself so complacently between the two of us." "There is a man," the others thought, "who ardently speaks about his partner's sterling character."

A timid but beautiful creature spoke up then, Miss Floral Arrangement. Being very artificial, she gave a most flowery speech, which seemed to be very much in keeping with her long stems which she knew how to display so effectively.

It was then that Mr. Kennel made his presence barkingly known. In his opinion, the country was going to the dogs. He also said that the cats (who, by the way, were having a protest march around the gates) should be let in. "Their meow should be heard," he said. "After all, this is a free country and we are entitled to a free-for-all."

By his hand motion, one could tell that the representative of the Supreme Court wanted to toot his horn. (He was in charge of parking the automobiles.) He reminded the gathering that there must be order, that the Cads and the Mustangs belong outside, the Birds, like the Thunderbirds and the dogs, inside. "This is the proper way in a democratic society," he screamed.

Time had sneaked in uninvited. Unobtrousively, she rested her face on the chairman's arm. He looked at her underhandedness in a most embarassed manner, she seemingly going into hiding at the stroke of twelve.

Needless to say, with that the meeting adjourned.

Birthday

Some Thoughts on the Congratulations
Received on my 75th Birthday

What is a birthday? Is it not really a day when one's own mother should be celebrated and not the new earthling?

It was she who created us and suffered for us in the process. Granted, it commemorates a date and, like the rings around the body of a tree, it is the event of the reoccurance which we count.

Mentally at least, just as we do on the first day of a new year, we draw a line under the account of the year gone by and evaluate its success or failure, not only in the material sense but spiritually as well. Whatever the result, life goes on and by this time (hopefully) we have learned to accept what is.

My consolation has always been that even the rich man can sleep in only one bed (at least at one time) and can only devour one breakfast, lunch and dinner a day. In other words, the measure of success is arbitrary. The tax collector is the one who enjoys success for sure and maybe the heirs, but as for oneself… where we are destined to go, the almighty dollar has no power. As far as I know, this is the only trip around and therefore the smartest thing one can do is to enjoy the journey to the fullest.

To that I drink and in that spirit I accept your felicitations.

Medals and Medallions

"Julius, my friend, I have two daughters who are going to be married soon and I want to give them a nice present of jewelry, something that will be a keepsake. What suggestion do you have?"

A probable conversation like this took place about a hundred years ago and they settled on two black onyx medallions, each with a beautiful pearl set in the middle. On the back was enough room to insert a small picture.

Lots of things have happened in Germany since this transaction took place. In the year of 1871, Germany won the war with France. The period between that war and the First World War in 1914 was a very prosperous one. It was the beginning of the Industrial Revolution and with that, the Jews in Germany experienced a fairly peaceful time. There existed what was known as "Salon Anti-Semitism," but no catastrophical happenings occurred and therefore the undercurrent of antagonistic expressions made no serious impact. The "Zentral Verein Deutscher Juden," comparable to the Anti-Defamation League in America, was able to keep matters under control. The Jews felt comfortable; they put their nationalism first and their religious affiliation second.

When war broke out in 1914 under Kaiser Wilhelm II, now known as World War I, the German Jews fought the war as patriotic Germans. They bought war bonds and saw to it that their sons enlisted in the army in order to defend their fatherland. Many of them died in the service of their country.

The spoils of war, winning or losing, are the medals placed upon the breasts of the soldier's uniforms, thus indicating that the fatherland is proud of their valor, courage, bravery and fearlessness. The German Jews cherished them with equal pride.

After four years of intensive fighting, World War I was lost. In the year of 1918, Germany signed a peace treaty in Versailles, France. The economic situation in Germany was dismal. In the 1920's, the country experienced an inflation, the likes of which had never been seen before. One billion marks was finally stabilized with one new mark. One can well imagine what effect such drastic action had on the burghers of Germany. They could not blame Kaiser Wilhelm II, who conveniently fled to neighboring Holland, where he lived withdrawn from all political activity until the day of his death. Who else can be blamed? You guessed it: the Jews. When the economy of a country is in shambles, the Jews get blamed. They are Capitalists and Communists at the same time. To haters, this makes absolutely no difference.

It was in this climate that Hitler came to the fore. By now, Germany had become a democracy and even though Hitler was put in jail for his detrimental activities, he was soon released and his activities went unreprimanded.

He wrote the book, *Mein Kampf,* in which he outlined to the tiniest detail his plans regarding the Jews. They did not read it.

Hitler raved and ranted for about ten years before he became Reichskanzler in 1933. The Jews heard it and saw it in print, but paid no heed. Life was still livable and they did not want to uproot and go somewhere else. The Jews, at least the majority of them, were deaf and blind to what was going on right under their unsmelling noses.

The Thousand-Year Reich lasted from 1933 to 1945, twelve horrible years. Finally, up until 1939, some of the German Jews went to Belgium, Holland and France, thinking that they would be safe. Unfortunately, Hitler was only playing a cat and mouse game with them. When he invaded these countries, the Jews were caught there. The countries in the eastern part of Europe did not have as much warning time and therefore the Jews in Austria, Poland, Hungary, Czechoslovakia and others were even worse off.

The irony of the whole disaster, now known as the Holocaust, is that the Jews of Europe unwittingly fueled the war machine of the Nazis. These sub-humans, who proclaimed themselves as the "Super Race," were nothing but a bunch of hoodlums, robbers and murderers. First they took the livelihoods of the Jews, then their possessions and finally their very lives. They killed six million Jews without the blink of an eye.

The medals which the Jewish soldiers had earned only twenty years earlier turned into nothing more than scrap-metal.

As time went on, the whole world, with very few exceptions, sealed itself off from the plight of the Jews. Shiploads of them, refugees, tried to obtain entry into Palestine, ruled by the British at that time, and into the United States of America, a declared democracy, but without success. America has come a long way. Cubans and Vietnamese, who found themselves in similar circumstances many years later, were permitted entry here. Even people who live in this country illegally for more than five years are granted amnesty. Had this only been the case then!

Oh, how quickly we forget. Israel was created as a safe haven for Jews from all over the world. It is our land, yours and mine. It is the only country in the world where a Hitler would have no chance.

My family and I came to the United States from Holland in 1937, where I had moved from Germany in 1933. We lived in Pittsburgh, Pennsylvania for ten years and moved to Portland, Oregon, in 1946, now more than fifty years ago. We learned that a branch of my wife's family also had settled in Portland, after leaving Germany. We met and have been close ever since.

Recently we gathered at an anniversary celebration of a mutual friend of ours. My wife wore her cherished medallion, black onyx with a pearl set in the center. This was given to her by her mother, but she knew that it came from her father's family. Our relative and friend wore hers on the same evening, the one which her mother had given her. She too knew that it originally came from her father's side. Thus they were able to reconstruct the history of these medallions. It took fifty years and many miles to come to fruition.

May the time not be distant when medals will eliminate themselves by peace throughout the world and medallions will continue to bring back to life fond memories of family history.

Atossah Lavender, The Cat's Meow

Dearest Mother Hadassah:

I have been meditating, while being comfortably stretched out under Father Hadassah Associate's garden chair, that I should send a greeting to you and to all the courageous Hadassah women who left their pets in the care of their husbands, hopefully Hadassah Associates too.

Mr. Lavender tells me that the organization after which you named me is composed of a particular species of women, people who feel, like every woman should, compassionate and endowed with a soft Jewish heart.

Come to think of it, I had a homeland once too, a place which we could call our own: Siam. Some of my best friends come from there. Even though I am very happy living with you in America, once in a while that instinctive feeling of my heritage comes through. In my world, we have similar problems as you have. We try to live in peace, but there is always some troublemaker. Take the Russian Wolfhound, a very graceful, smooth animal, but he is also sleek and we have to be very careful. I heard him speak of "Detante," but I wonder if this did not come from his friend, a German Shepherd who was speaking of "Die Tante," and that Russian got it all mixed up.

The Cat People too have gone through various stages in history. In ancient Rome, we were the symbol of liberty. In the Middle Ages, we had a very bad time; Pope Innocent VIII in the fifteenth century saw cat worship as a link with the devil. So you see, just like you, we have had our problems. Fortunately you have one advantage; you speak and can be understood; while we too speak, we are hardly ever understood. It is my wish that from your meeting, the idea of "understanding" will fly on wings of peace throughout the Middle East.

When the Arabs speak of the "Zionist Conspiracy," I wonder if it is the fact that, maybe, they have heard of Hadassah, the conspiracy of American women to bring peace, good health and contentment not only to the Middle East, but to the whole world.

I don't want to overstay my cat's welcome, but I simply had to tell you how proud I am to have my stenographer as a Hadassah Associate and you, my boss, as a Hadassah Mother.

May peace become the world's cat's meow.

Yours,
Atossah

The Prostrated Prostate

The privilege of being MALE requires our paying the necessary dues. In case of war, we have to put our life on the line and in the battle of the sexes, it is *"vive la difference."*

It was at 6:30 AM when I obediently reported to the Urology Department of the hospital. There they blatantly confiscated my clothes and left me naked upon the bed. Vultures, who sucked my blood, fell over me, then plied me with pills before they rolled me onto the operating table. Here I was injected with a local anesthesia, which gradually numbed me from the navel down to my toes. While the doctors worked behind a screen, I chatted amiably with the anesthesist sitting behind me. After one and a half hours, I was told that the operation was completed. In all honesty, I was not even conscious of the fact that they had started.

Now I was rolled to the Recovery Room. Here I touched my sides for the first time. They felt like the blubber of a whale. Luckily no fins had grown. Nurses were flitting about, once again taking my blood pressure, temperature and pulse. Gradually the drug wore off. The first movement occurred in my left foot. Only very slowly, limbs and toes unfroze like ice from a rooftop.

The first day, I was still chained to the I.V. and what I like to call the P.P., both of them being hung on a rolling stand. While taking my intermittent fifteen-minute walks, I navigated it and myself along the enclosed balcony which surrounds the building. It is here in the rooms adjoining where you find the huddled masses yearning to be free.

In what way differ the nights from the days? During the waking hours, you get all possible attention from the nurses and doctors. At night, when you like to be left alone, it seems that the night nurse enters the room only after you finally have fallen asleep and wakes you up to offer you a sleeping pill. While at it, she naturally takes your blood pressure, your pulse and your temperature.

The removal of the catheter certainly was not the most pleasant sensation nor is being used as a pin-cushion the most desired spot in which one can find oneself.

Every man wants to be "William The Conquerer," or whatever his first name might be. The thought of knighthood in flower seems to stay with us throughout our lives. What steed would want to be a gelding?

Enough on this subject. Let us put a fig leaf over it!

The Standard Bearer

There she was, this remarkable woman, who, only yesterday it seems, was a child herself.

Suddenly she was faced with the full responsibility in which situation a young woman finds herself when she is in the process of entering the bond of marriage. Were she to explain the reasons why she fell in love with this particular young man, she would indeed be at a loss for words. By the mystique given only to the female of the species, he proposed to her and she accepted him...that was not really under question.

Often, while budding into young womanhood, she had mulled over in her mind the role she might someday be chosen to play.

Hers now was the most responsible position in the country. Dive into it, she said to herself, just like into a swimming pool and keep on swimming.

From her husband's remarks, however, only after she had carefully invited them, ("Do you like my cooking tonight?" "Yes, I do!") she built her own strong defenses. Often there were indeed kind glances in her direction from which she drew the strength to be the hostess in the home, chief cook in the kitchen, grand dame in the boudoir, first lady in the company of others and, most of all, mother to her children.

Though each child calls some male his father, it is the mother who bears the burden, feeding and clothing the children, educating them, leading them onto the path of life.

My wife.

To Our Children, To Anyone's Children

"I did not ask you to put me into this world!"

What parent has not heard these words out of the mouth of a child at a time of disagreement?

Parents, in a sense, are overgrown children. Where is the dividing line? Some children have children when they are twelve years old.

If you want to drive a car, you must first learn how and then pass a driver's test. Theoretically, when you want to have a child, you should earn a license to do so, proving that you not only have the knowledge of how to go about it, but also how to be able to bring up such a living creature, how to sustain it. This is not only in your own interest, but also in that of the child and the society in which you both live. As you can well see, since this is neither required nor possible, I must add, the problem remains.

Now to my children and yours who, in all probability were brought up in a similar fashion far removed from the status with which I opened this discourse. Remember when they were born, the pleasure of dapper diapering? How quickly they grew up to go to school. One purpose seemed to be to bring home colds which they had caught there. Was it only yesterday when you helped them with their school assignments, the chauffering you had to do to bring them to their various after-school activities? It was a chore, but we loved it.

All too fast, they grew up. They went to college to further their education, maybe to learn a trade and, last but not least, for your daughter to find a husband, preferably a future doctor or lawyer. (Strange, we really do not send boys to college to find a wife. We prefer that they abstain from such a venture, at least for a time.)

Let us assume that your and my children are married now, even though the probability has decreased substantially by the modern practice of "shacking-up." No marriage license, no commitment needed and all the benefits which used to be unavailable without marriage in the old days. What a deal! Or is it?

Assume that they were lucky enough to get married. What yesterday was wine, roses and dancing, changed into obligations. That is quite a transition. With ambitions come hardships, all part of making a life and love. Maybe the husband still goes to college to earn a degree; therefore, in all probablility, the wife has to go out to earn the bread and kosher bacon. In spite of the excellent food available today, the value of meals on the run cannot be compared to those of say thirty years ago. This food seems to bring about only larger bodies in size, but not in the stamina with which older generations seemingly are blessed. Youth today, I believe, is eternally tired, something which even sleep cannot wipe out. Granted, the mental strain is greater than it was years ago, so much more has to be learned to obtain "that shingle," which opens the door to financial success.

There are only three major occurances in a person's life of which marriage is the only consciously taken one; the other two, birth and death, are foisted upon us. Being newly married brings a tremendous amount of adjustments: for the boy to wean himself from the breast of his mother and for the girl to separate herself from the psychological marriage with her father. Suddenly courtship, this dream-like period in a person's life, becomes actually living with that stranger beside you. You have to continue to prove the love you professed to have for each other in every word and action. When actually living with one another, seeing sides which were hidden as if on the other side of the moon and are now suddenly spotlighted, Lovey-Dovey becomes Learney-Earney.

Lugging food to the table for breakfast, lunch and dinner also means washing dishes. The stunning outfit you so admired on her becomes her reponsibility to wash, to dry clean, to iron, to hang away. Then there is the bed, this Four Poster, which plays such an important role in the history of mankind. Two entirely different species, people of different make-up, character, likes and dislikes, suddenly pounce upon each other, hoping to find Paradise on Earth. Paradise can turn out to be just a garden with overgrown weeds and, sometimes, Dante's Inferno itself.

Often young couples do not realize that in courtship one

gives while the other receives. In marriage, it becomes a give-and-take situation and often one must take more than they can humanly bear. Education does not end when one leaves home or school and marriage indeed is an extension course, to be taken not just during the summer, but all through life. One has to learn how to take or change likes and dislikes, how to communicate without raising voices and how to temper tempers.

The words, "I love you," can be bought on a card from the Five & Dime Store. To act upon them at all times, to put them into action, is a continuous process. The secret to be discovered is that love means giving of oneself, and when two people give, give, give, years later they will find out by this miracle which love bears within itself that they have become recipients, takers, in the form of the glow of happiness. "I love you" means "I want to give you happiness."

That this message has not been fully understood is proven by the fact that two-thirds of marriages are shipwrecked on the rock of stubborness. The only force at work is divorce. But is it a solution? Actually one set of problems gets exchanged for another. No matter what, he or she was a warm body, companionship. Now you look at empty space. Whatever has to be done, it is you who has to do it; there is no George to call to take out the garbage. If there are children, it is the female who probably has to take care of them. It is up to her to educate them, which means it is you who has to be tough with them at times. He, the male butterfly, who probably nipped on another flower long ago, has visiting rights. This is usually on Sunday when he can take the kids to a movie, to the zoo, all the wonderful places that kids dream of going. He is the fun-giver and, particularly in the early years, you are the "I hate you, Mom!" Sad, but true.

What am I writing here? A sex manual for *Playboy*?

Part III
Love

Why All But One?

If you want to buy merchandise, you walk into a store and do so.

If you want to build a house, you see a contractor and you come to an agreement.

If you want to arrange for a cemetary lot, you may do so even though your body is still warm.

The most difficult problem to solve is to go shopping for a husband.

If you smile at a man on the street, he thinks that you are fresh.

If you don't smile at that same man, he won't know that you are alive.

If you do overcome your shyness and put your elbow into him, you immediately find that you should not have done it because he is not your type.

I believe that it would be a very wise custom for girls to wear little markers like:

I am free.
Look me over!
How about it?

Anything to make matters easier for eyes seemingly fashioned to look...but never to see.

DREAM

Who are you, man or woman,
Fact or fiction,
Transplanting me on magic wings
Upon a planet where wish becomes fulfillment
And reality puts on a filmy gown?

Am I you, are you I, are we one
Vision or reflection?
Are we at all?

Eyes which see when closed,
Ears which hear words unsaid,
The mind which travels miles in a second
And thus makes distance nearness,
Opposites equals.

Is what I experience
A vapor trail from the past
Or a glance, maybe, into Tomorrow-land?

Imagination and image, yes, you are one.
Just as He, who created you and me.

CHARM

Charm is like the facet of a diamond,
Reflecting perfection,
Clearness of the bearer's soul.

Charm transmits itself in a twinkle of the eye,
A movement of the hand, a smile upon the face.

Charm is fascination, essence,
Flavor, final touch,
Intoxication upon man's senses,
Freeing him from freedom,
Enslaving him, ever so lovingly.

EMOTIONS

Emotions foam like the waves
Of the ocean,
And they reach many times
Their height.
With the break of the waves,
They spend themselves in vain.

Fill your life with oceans of emotions.
The break of the wave will reach
The periphery of Heaven and Earth,
And foam gently caressing the shore
Will be their only character witness.

The Statue in the Park

No one really knows how long she has stood there on a pedestal, the Goddess of Love. No one really knew who had sculptured her; she simply was there, always, admired by each passerby, young and old, giving to each a different impression though she herself never changed, standing there in her unparalleled beauty, unadorned, being what she was meant to be – Nature in her most natural form.

One hot summer night, through the shadow of the swaying trees animated by the whisper of the cooling wind, there walked a man, young and pure. An artist he was, a writer, who walked here with a dream, the dream that someday he would find her, his image, transfixed there in his mind, she who was beyond all human description, ethereal, unreachable it seemed. Many a maiden had tried to touch his heart, to stir his soul; all he had ever left for them was a sad look of disappointment. He too, as many had done before him, stood at the foot of the statue of the Goddess of Love. Awed by her beauty, he knelt down and kissed her foot. He noticed that even her toes were intricately, beautifully shaped. As his kiss reached the stone, a tear fell from his eye and at that very moment he felt warmth upon his lips and a slight stir.

In wonder he looked up and saw a smile upon her face, a hand outstretched, which seemed to beg: Please help me down. Only now he saw her in full beauty, a body divine, just as he had envisioned it in his dreams, a face which unleashed a thousand emotions within him. Her flowing light hair, so beautifully long, caressed his cheek.

She said to him, "Oh, how very long have I been waiting for you, the one person in the world who still has a heart, who can still sacrifice a tear, a tear of love!"

Arm in arm, they walked away, into each other's heart and soul.

Mr. Mountain and Miss Lake

*Written at Timberline Lodge in view of Mount Hood
and Lost Lake, Oregon*

Hello there, beautiful Miss Lake! I have been standing here for God only knows how long without ever paying attention to you, who must have been situated there equally as long. Somehow, it seems, we get involved with ourselves and, come to think of it, I have been looking up mostly and had my head in the clouds. There was a time when I was full of life and lava. Every so often, I would blow my top and cause havoc, but I have quieted down a great deal. Since I am more concrete than the heavens above me, man started to worship me like a god. They are funny people in so far as I can judge from here. What do you think? They always want to reach the top of me, to reach beyond themselves. No matter what my physical condition – covered with snow, frozen by ice, surrounded by howling winds – up they come. Some make it, some fall off my cliffs. The warmest bed I can give them are my snow-blanketed caverns.

But why am I telling you all about this? It is a beautiful day, the sun is out and even an old mountain like me feels emotional. Just the other day, I happened to look down for a change. It was a clear day too, no clouds, no fog to hamper my vision, and I saw you there, lying so very still, so beautiful. How charmingly blue you are, how clear, how quiet, how serene. My friends, the snowflakes, tell me that you are really part of them; that when spring comes, it is they who melt, roll down my back in heavy streams and join you as one. It is hard for me to believe that all the whiteness they display up here turns into such blue upon touching you. You know, Miss Lake (and I believe that this is what you are, must be, only can be), I like you. Where I am rough and tough, you are smooth, soft and gentle. Where I seem majestic, you appear quiet and pensive. Where I have height, you have depth. My reflection within you seems to reach far, far down and yet, I can feel that there are regions within you far, far deeper than I can imagine. Can it really be that my power, my majesty is only as great as you, my humble friend, permit me to absorb? Even though I, the strong one, supposedly have the powers of Heaven, even though often it is thought that in mere physical strength lies ultimate achievement, it is you – I can see it now so clearly – you by your magnitude, by your passive absorption, are indeed the world's wonderment.

Oh, time, how beautiful art thou, how kind, placing the two of us so close. The elements create the connecting link between us, my tears, which you absorb and give back to me in the form of a mystic veil, rising up to me, embracing me. In this act of transformation lies the value to our very being, to our existence. To conquer is to yield.

What is a mountain without a lake?

What is a man without the woman he loves?

I SAT IN NATURE'S LAP

Yes, I sat in Nature's Lap,

This fertile Woman

Who with her misty eyes

Kissed me and the morning.

She spoke in a language unknown,

And yet I felt the web of time,

Weaving like a brook its way unshown.

How young and fresh are her airs,

As majestic as the wonders of a tree.

With her hand upon my head she sang to me.

I felt so cozy at her bosom,

So filled with mystery,

The World and her cares here did not blossom,

The triller of her voice did silence me.

Man forbidden, she seemed to say,

Let him conquer the Earth,

It does not matter, it is I who conquers him.

Thus she put her arms about me,

And I fell asleep for all Eternity.

SPIRITUOSO

A sprite sprang graciously
Through Spring,
Spirited by Ecstacy.

And this is that wondrous thing.
Thus, she became "Esprit."

Part IV
America

What Makes an American a Great American?

The very first question an American puts before a newcomer, even if he hardly has time to put his feet on American soil, is, "How do you like America?" Speaking about America is a much more intricate problem than a pointed question to which the answer can only be yes or no.

Under the immigration law, any man, woman or child, once admitted into this country, can receive citizenship papers after five years of residence, provided that they are classified as loyal. Where else in the world can you become a citizen so easily and, I might also point out, as advantageously? Holland, for example, where I resided for several years, grants citizenship after payment of several thousand gulden, this being possible only after a required residence of ten years. While in many countries only money will buy citizenship, here in America, plain loyalty does it...plus a few bucks to cover administrative expenses. How unbelievably idyllic to become part of the finest country on earth where the admission price is loyalty alone.

What makes an American a great American? In my opinion, one of the basic factors is that the American people are not the result of a great melting pot, as has so often been claimed, but rather of a more modern method of cooking, the steam cooker. In the melting pot, materials melt into one product, losing all resemblance to their former shapes. In a steam cooker, however, steam is produced, the American ideal will puff out but the basic flavors of various nationalities, religions, races and traditions will remain. It is here that the greatness of the American ideal lies: merging the soul, but leaving the physical heritage intact.

When you look into American history, into the history of her great men, you will find that they are remembered not so much by their achievements as by their great human action. Take Abraham Lincoln, as an example, the most humble American who ever lived in spite of his achievements. His human character and the greatness of his thoughts and deeds will keep his memory alive as long as there are Americans.

Turning the wheel of time back several more years, we think of Thomas Jefferson, the man who penned the Declaration of Independence. The battle cry of his time was "life, liberty and prosperity." By changing one single word – prosperity – into "the pursuit of happiness" and by incorporating this changed and improved thought in the Declaration, he gave us the mental makeup of our present time.

Let's talk for a moment of the great Americans of the twentieth century. Let us think of the people who are still enslaved or of martyrs willing to die for the cause of a free world. They all are great Americans, I might say, even if they have never seen America. The idea of being an American, a great American, is nothing less than being a human being, a being humane. Yes, such people do not live in the Western Hemisphere alone. I sincerely hope that they will emerge from their struggle soon as fundamental pillars of democracy all over the world and mingle in the steam of American thought.

To achieve all of this, we need leaders whose feelings go far beyond nationalism, men for whom the American ideal is not empty phrasiology. These men must be able to raise the standard of living for people all over the world. Human actions have the traits of a boomerang: good deeds airborne come flying back adorned with the olive branch of peace. Reparations, retaliations and hatred can only plant the seeds of war.

Tremendous tasks lie before us. Let all of us participate in their solutions. Let us approach them not with the air of superiority, but in all humility. The cry of the humble will then become a roar, bringing peace to all of the world.

Clothes Make Politics

Often I have wondered if the world would not be in better shape were our politicians to wear the garb of Ghandi, a simple white sheet. This attire, with red flannel underwear added on cold days, would remind our senators and representatives that theirs is the most responsible job to be administered in the country and that our future depends on the wisdom of their actions.

I cannot imagine that any of these men could act overbearing and smug were we to view them on our color television sets garbed in that attire. Our leaders, I believe, would come down to earth once more and enact more and better legislation which we, the earthworms, need to keep on crawling.

My Son, The American

Yes, it happened yesterday. Over and over I had measured the square footage of the waiting room which adjoined the delivery room of the Montefiore Hospital in Pittsburgh, Pennsylvania, where my wife was in the process of bringing into this world an American child. Finally, exhausted, I fell asleep in one of those comfortable armchairs. The atmosphere changed. I sensed myself in conversation with the baby...

"Howdy, Pop," the child addressed me.

"How do you do, my boy," I inquired.

"Come on, Old Man, don't be so formal," the son of mine said. "I feel like a newborn baby, if you ask me. But why talk about me? It looks as if you are the one who needs some attention right now."

"No, not at all," I replied, flabbergasted. "I am feeling fine. Do not worry about me. No father was ever lost yet in the act of becoming a father. But I would like to welcome you as a new member of our family, small as it is. I hope that you will like your mother and father."

"By the way," my son remarked, "something must be done about your accent. You speak exactly like Charles Boyer, an asset no doubt on the stage, but not highly valued in the world you live in. Your clothes need some improvement too. No civilized American wears a necktie on Sunday."

"Where are we?" I said to myself. "Where did I hear that voice before?"

"Is there something I can do for you, my son?" I asked him.

"Keep your diaper on, Old Man," I suddenly heard him say laughingly." Tell me, what is the divorce rate at the present time and how is America making out in the world situation?"

"Listen, you are driving me toward two dangerous subjects, psychology and politics," I said. "What we actually should be talking about are parables and fables, thus learning from the past and maybe phrenology to get a look into your future. How about a drink? I am awfully thirsty."

"Let's have a good steak with it and a game of cards afterwards. At the same time, we can listen to the football game over the radio," he said.

And that is exactly what happened. While we lifted our glasses, I said, *"Honi soit qui mal y pense!"* The boy laughed, not knowing what I said, but sensing the meaning. We both knew that we were made for each other.

When I finally woke up, the doctor told me that I was the father of a lovely baby girl.

New York Life

New York life rolls off before one's eyes like an ever changing ocean. Everything and everybody is pushing. Automobiles, droschkes, trucks, people, orientals and occidentals, accidentals and incidentals. New York is like a merry-go-round which whirls without end. Some of the movement is up, some down, but always movement. The rhythm is that of a pulse continually beating, pushing and pressing the life blood into all the various traffic arteries. Some people go to work, some to play, some to live, some to die, but the drive, the impulse, remains. Heartache and sorrow, joy and happiness, all of these emotions are mixed like a deck of cards. The Queen of Hearts, the Joker...only fate knows what is up.

But it is New York life. It is living. It is the breath of God.

Fame and Fate

Great men, it seems, always have to pay a great price for the brilliant mind with which God has endowed them. From the dull thrust of a dagger into Caesar to the Dallas thrall who, with the markmanship taught him in the Marine Corps, wiped out his Supreme Commander. Every man has illusions of grandeur, this assinine assassin included, who had chosen this evil pass to guide him to the most abominable fame. A great man like John F. Kennedy, who had survived the most insidious attacks by a Pacific enemy, simply could not be hampered, nor pampered, by a protective bubble on his tour of good will. How can you convince a crowd of people of your straight-forward intentions from behind a shield which belies everything you are? These must have been the feelings which caused the President to ride through the streets of Dallas, Texas, unprotected, as proved to be the case.

It is frightening indeed that a little bullet can so drastically alter the ballot of time. Men in office have been assassinated before, but never so young and vigorous a one who was the symbol of youth, of life. A bullet felled Abraham Lincoln, America's First Emancipator, bringing about a chain reaction of exploding gunpowder which, to this day, a hundred years later, is still combusting and has now claimed America's Second Emancipator, John F. Kennedy. We may say proudly that we are living in the twentieth century, meaning that we have come a long way. What a delusion. We have hardly stepped out of the shell of ignorance, living in a world where might still rules right in every one of its phases. It is these two basic factors which rule the mind of man, the righteous and the mightiness. What the righteous tried to achieve with the power of the mind, mightiness can easily wipe out with the single pull of a trigger, an alignment of battle confrontation which spells the loser clearly from the start.

A three-year-old son salutes his father. It is we whom he symbolizes, saluting our dead President onto his last journey.

Not an iota more do we know than this little man of three years of age as to the whys and wherefores of this needless spectacle. While we pledge ourselves at this sad moment to improve, to do better, to learn, we learn not. There is no sense of responsibility in us stronger and more deeply rooted than in this fatherless child. Yes, this little man is the symbol of our great melodrama in which all of us American people find ourselves inextricably enmeshed.

Part V
Religion

PRAYER

Prayer is the transfiguration of loneliness

Into aloneness with God.

Thoughts reel back, remembrance is reflected

On the screen of the mind.

Father, Mother pass by our souls

Like clouds of mist at crack of dawn.

Yesterday, that kneadable material into which we wove

Hope, goodness, work, curses, thanks,

We tried to create, to educate, to shape, we....

Night comes, we lie down and eradicate.

Again we are alone and we remain

Alone with God,

Man's only Prerogative.

Holy Day

Carillion tunes coming from a nearby church tower inter-
mingled with the heavy ding-dong of a competitive church
across the hills awaken me this morning. Call it what you may-
Merry Christmas, Happy Hanukkah – the purpose is the same.

My oldest daughter, Eleonore, has gifted me with writing
paper; my youngest daughter, Fay, has surprised me with ink;
the co-workers I spend my time with the year around in an
effort to make an honest living have provided the penholder and
pen as a special gift to their boss. My beloved wife has pur-
chased the desk on which to rest all of these utensils with many
more hidden in the drawers. I am to furnish the thoughts to fill
the paper, to use the ink and to make the purchase of the desk
worthwhile.

This season to me has always been like a day of reckoning.
All during the month of December, I rack my brain to decide
what to give to the members of my family and whom to write to
this year; who should be added to the circle of my friends and
who is to be eliminated. (They and the forgotten friends always
show up on the holiday in the most faithful manner.) Somehow
it seems to be the day when I like to sit down to put a line under
the yearly account headed: What kind of life have you led this
year? The question mark generally stands out as the most tangi-
ble factor, influencing the words under the line.

The spirit of the season is interpreted in many ways. Some
take it internally and answer to themselves. Others search their
souls; they go to church or synagogue, visit sick friends, do all
the things all of us should do all year around every day, but do
not because we say to ourselves that we do not have the time.
Actually, we could find the time if we only wanted to. Deep
down, we do not really want to. As a last resort, we have
reserved one day of the year for this purpose, one day to white-
wash ourselves from our year-round omittances.

The magnitude and the magnificence of the world, the
minute kernel of sand which, nevertheless, has exacting shape,

our strife and our indifference are all part of the most precious gift, life itself; a gift only lent to us for a short period of time to give us the opportunity to show what we are able to do with it. Unlike other gifts, it has to be returned to its Maker.

Yom Kippur

When the melody of the Kol Nidre touched my Jewish heart, I searched for an interpretation of my own. I saw myself walking on a road leading from a beautiful valley where streams gently flow. Fern, that eternal plant, graces its sides. I, however, am walking upwards, against the current in a gradual ascent. No humans can be heard or seen; only the voice of Nature is felt in her eloquent way: crickets chirping, the brook splashing, leaves whispering and birds proclaiming the glory of the sky above them by their endless song. In this utterly peaceful setting, there was I. I felt deeply that I was part of that Nature, one of her messengers trying to fulfill her purpose. No clear and precise message is entrusted to me, only the road straight ahead and before me. The goal up there upon the hilltop and beyond is shrouded in a cloud. Very, very slowly, I progress through the impressive beauty which surrounds me. The mystic impact which is about me cannot be lessened by probing, be it with shovel or analytical mind. Science, religion, they are all trying to explain, yet cannot really tell what it is that moves the vocal cord or the muscle of a finger which holds a pen. Still, I walk upwards, firmly because faith and confidence prove to be stronger than gigantic dams, walls and bridges made of steel and stone. Knowing this, I easily reach the top of the mountain in my sojourn, while the last bars of the Kol Nidre glide into the beyond, where peace, eternal peace, is waiting.

Hanukkah, The Festival of Lights

This inspiring holiday prompts me to interpret the individual lights the way I see them:

The Knight – He, who brings light to all of the eight representatives symbolized on the menorah.

The Bright – He, who represents the sparkle, the brilliance of life, the spirit which moves us.

The Might – The strength we receive from keeping alive this tradition, this example we set for our children, this custom which our fathers instilled in us.

The Right – To defend our principles, in work and in action, to do that which is right in our eyes, protecting our interests as well as those of others.

The Fight – Here I think of Israel, our spiritual homeland, physical refuge for many of our brethren, this valiant country of enlightenment which has to battle an unfeeling and hating world.

The Sight – The vision that the Jewish people have of a better world where diverse people can live together.

The Flight – Gathering thousands of people under the protective wing of the Americas and Israel. Even though many people were not granted this life-saving event, right now we are involved in trying to free 400,000 Russian Jews from their enslavement.

The Plight – The sound resolve to work for a better, more peaceful world, hoping that someday the United Nations will be a uniter of nations, a savior.

The Blight – The decay we see all around us, poverty and hunger, lawlessness from the highest circles on down, greed that far outweighs need.

And yet...and yet, through centuries we have kindled the lights in hope that someday peace will reign on earth. Oh yes, the highest achievement is: to get along.

A Personal Invitation to Visit Israel

By Edith R. Lavender

Have you ever reached a decision in half an hour to travel eight thousand miles away? I did when I received a letter in June, 1973, from the National Tourism Department of Hadassah, signed by its chairman, Mrs. Israel Usdan. It offered two weeks of intensive study of Israel, her people, institutions, cities and monuments and whatever else could be of interest at the very special rate of $699. This included literally everything: first class hotels, three meals per day, transfers, a private air-conditioned coach and a most enjoyable sightseeing trip through Israel with a charming guide named Itzhak and a good-looking driver, Mordechai.

At first, my husband, Paul, thought that I was out of my mind when I announced that I would leave in a couple of weeks for such a tour, but he also was convinced once he read the letter. And so I signed up and made my reservations via United Air Lines to meet with the other ladies in New York, after leaving Portland, Oregon, on the morning of Sunday, June 3.

The excitement started when I reached the El Al Terminal at Kennedy Airport and met some of the other Hadassah members. As it is with all groups, everyone tried very cautiously to "sniff each other out," if you know what I mean. I had been assigned to Group #1, thirty-seven ladies and some husbands, all from New York and surrounding area. I was very upset because there were Hadassah members from all over the United States taking part in this tour and some nitwit had assigned me to travel all of the time with the girls from New York. Far be it from me to dislike New Yorkers, but I would have liked to meet and sit once in a while with ladies from somewhere else! Thus, I made my objections known in no uncertain terms and as it turned out, it did me no good at all; once assigned, there was no way of changing it. In all honesty, I found wonderful people and good friends right in my own group. We also had plenty of opportu-

86

nity to get acquainted with the others in the first week since we were all staying at the same hotel during our lodging in Jerusalem.

We boarded our 747 El Al Jet and off we flew with a stopover in London, where we had a long delay. Service and personnel were first class and everytime I dozed off, someone woke me with the very happy news that they were serving another nourishing tidbit. We reached LOD Airport at 6:00 PM Israeli time, Monday, June 4. For most of us, it was the first time we had set foot in our ancient homeland. It was my second time, having been there for three weeks in 1963 with my daughter, Fay Toni, but how everything had changed! I got the impression right from the start of how much the country had grown and developed.

While in Jerusalem, we stayed at the Hotel Diplomat. Actually, we were slated to occupy rooms at the famous King David Hotel, which would have been nicer because it is more centrally located, but here is where our "villain" stepped in (every interesting story has to have at least one) by the name of Chancellor Willie Brandt of Germany. Yes, our visit coincided with this famous man and did we find that out right away. Now I don't suppose that he had any inkling of our group, but he proved to be the proverbial millstone around our neck, as you will see if you stay awake long enough to finish this *"megillah."*

The Diplomat Hotel is a very new one, richly decorated with beautiful murals, mosaics, exquisite paintings and with a large lobby, bar, banquet and dining rooms. Our accommodations were lovely and I was also very lucky by having assigned to me a charming roommate, Mrs. Edith Schulman, from New York. During our two-week stay, we always roomed together and we got along famously. We clicked immediately, took care of each other, forgave each other our weaknesses and thus tried to make our stay in Israel even more enjoyable. I know that I was very content with this charming, attractive lady, wearing lovely clothes and also appreciative of the fact that she did not smoke. I simply could not have roomed with some of the others who were never without their cigarettes. Edith had a twenty-three year-old daughter living in Tel-Aviv, who visited us several times and brought her *Sabra*-boyfriend along. In fact, they got engaged and I hope that despite big differences in upbringing and ideals, they will be very happy.

On our arrival, we found gifts from the hotel in our room, gorgeous flowers from the local Hadassah group, maps, postcards and, despite the late hour, we were served a nice dinner. The hotel is built right on the old borderline and has a magnificent view into the Judaen Hills. Most of the waiters and chambermaids were Arabs and I can only state that they were extremely friendly and courteous. I had some very interesting conversations with them; of course, I talk with everyone as I am the curious type.

Naturally, I am not going to report step-by-step what we did in Jerusalem, nor on our later tour of the country. I will touch on places and memories that seem to be important to me, experiences that I will never forget.

Our motorcoach prominently displayed a sign: Hadassah Board Member Tour #1. Our guide, Itzhak, and driver, Mordechai, stayed with us all the time. They took care of us, tried to make the travel interesting and we really got to know each other. I hope they will remember this particular Hadassah group with kindness.

To introduce us to the history of Jerusalem, we first visited a model, a reproduction, of the ancient walled city and temple in the time of Solomon, built to exact scale. By showing this to us, it helped later to identify archeological discoveries and the layout of the walled city.

Jerusalem is a very personal experience. It means so much to Jews and many other religions all over the world. Out of all the memories of these exciting days, I have picked these sights and impressions to share with you.

Vad Ya Schem The memorial for the six million murdered Jews under the Nazi regime. How can I describe what I felt? I have never forgotten, nor forgiven, and as long as I live, their memory will be with me – my people, my brothers and sisters, who were slaughtered by mericless killers. This memorial is a holy place to me.

Shrine Of The Scrolls I have always been attracted to the science of Archeology and when I heard about the discovery of the Dead Sea Scrolls in 1948-1949, I read all the material published about them; however, nothing makes the same impression as actually standing in front of the Dead Sea Scrolls themselves. The shrine looks like a spaceship from the outside and is even more overpowering, once you enter. You are on a ramp leading downwards, with displays explaining all the steps leading to the discovery in the Quamram Caves, their acquisition and the decipherment of the scrolls. How fascinating! I could have stayed there much longer.

The ancient city walls of Jerusalem have seen history rushing by for thousands of years. Ever since King David acquired this ancient site and Solomon built his temple here, conquerors have come and gone, torn down and rebuilt, and now the ancient city once more is under the rule of the Jews! Like pilgrims of old, we walked through a gate where a soldier looked through our handbags, across a forecourt and there it was, the Wailing Wall.

The Wailing Wall This is a huge, almost white wall divided into two sections, one for men, the other for women. Prayers are said here at all times, for twenty-four hours a day. You cover your head, approach the wall and ask yourself, "What are you, oh man, that God remembers you?" This is the greatest of emotional experiences and certainly a private moment for taking stock of yourself.

Later, we also visited the underground excavations around the temple and were told about new archaeological discoveries. On another day, we visited the Wailing Wall again, strolled around the old city, witnessing its vibrant, noisy life, the Arab inhabitants, their shops and bazaars, gazed at the Via Dolorosa and did a little shopping. Jerusalem, viewed from one of its hills, is a lovely golden city with new high-rise apartments everywhere. Metal cranes on top of half-finished buildings are almost trademarks and we were told that lots of Arabs find work on the construction sites. They are bussed in every day and make good wages. Still, there is a shortage of apartments and as far as renting is concerned, there are almost none because it is the custom here to buy your apartment. The prices are unbelievably high, $100,000 to $150,000, for a three-room apartment in Jerusalem or Tel-Aviv. Inflation is as bad there as it is here. This is especially hard on young couples, as they are unable to even raise the down payment without help.

Mt. Herzl and Mt. Zion On a mountain top overlooking the city he visualized, there is Herzl's grave in black marble, very simple. His body was brought from Vienna in 1948. Here also are the military cemetaries, stretching far; a sad place because you think of the sacrifice those young gallant men made for their beloved country.

Now I will tell you about our free days. As I mentioned before, the Diplomat was located a bit farther out of town and often we had to use taxis run by Arabs. On Moslem holidays the Jewish drivers take over.

I contacted my cousin, Annie Bodenheimer (born Rosenthal), before the holidays as she and her family are orthodox and do not answer the telephone nor drive on Shabbath or holidays. She invited me for dinner at 12:00 noon, after the men come home from services.

On Shevuouth morning, I first went to the Rockefeller Museum, which is inside the walled city near the Jaffa Gate, run by Arabs, and spent an enchanting two hours there. I was almost alone in this beautiful place formerly a Jordanian museum. One of the guides approached me and asked in his Oxfordian English if I were really interested in antiquities. When I answered in the affirmative, he took me on a private tour as he knew every nook and cranny. Later I took his picture and promised to send him a print.

Afterwards, I took another taxi to Annie's home, this after a considerable wait. I had a lovely time with Annie and her husband, Wolf, who is now retired, together with their daughter, Chava, her young husband and baby. Late in the afternoon, I returned to the hotel and took a swim in the large pool. After a delightful holiday dinner, the six of us decided to attend the Light and Sound Show, given nightly. Luckily, I took a blanket along because it can get chilly at night. The show was marvelous, a poetic interpretation of the history of Jerusalem set to fine music.

I have not mentioned before that Mrs. Israel Usdan, our National Chairman for Tourism, had personally prepared this trip for us. She went to Israel two weeks prior and greeted us very graciously. We saw her several times, particularly when she introduced the speakers at our banquets. She certainly worked very hard to make this tour an outstanding one.

Hebron An all Arab city formerly in Jordan, has an agreement with the government to let tour buses enter at certain times for the visit of Abraham's Tomb. This is located in the Cave of Machpela, mentioned in the Bible, and is a holy place to three religions. Abraham bought it to bury his wife, Sarai, and later on his son, Itzhak, as well as Jacob and Leah who also are supposedly buried there. Since Abraham was the father of Ishmael, son of Hagar, he is venerated by all Arabs as their forefather. Therefore, the graves are equally holy to them and they guard them jealously.

This was supposed to be the day we were to visit the Knesset, Israel's House of Parliament, a beautiful building sitting on a knoll overlooking Jerusalem. But our "nemesis" dogged us. Willie Brandt was there and therefore nobody else could get in. Even though we all had our passports with us, nothing prevailed and we never saw the inside of the Knesset.

There are a few places on this earth where one feels that one stands on holy ground. It has nothing to do with organized religion or to what deity prayers are sent heavenwards; the entire atmosphere is drenched with a stillness which proclaims that man can pass beyond his own limitations. The Acropolis in Athens, the Vatican in Rome, the Island of Delos (holy to Apollo), Stonehenge in England and, of course, the Wailing Wall in Jerusalem are among these sacred sites, but also the Dome of the Rock, holy to Islam must be included. This gorgeous golden-domed edifice stands inside the Walled City on Mt. Moria, where Abraham nearly sacrificed Isaac, near the place where Solomon built the temple. Inside, it is very simple, but rich with golden engravings from the Koran. There are rugs on the floor (we all had to take off our shoes), but otherwise it is empty. Yet, it is still very impressive and in beautiful condition. Of course, the Arabs are in charge of their mosques and holy places, just as the Christians (210 sects?) fight over their holy places, without interference from the Israeli Government.

While shopping in the downtown area in New Jerusalem, I also found some shoes I have been looking for ever since I left Germany in 1935. They are called "Gesundheits Schuhe" (Good Health Shoes). The man who owned the factory emigrated to Israel, opened a shoe factory and is selling these orthopedic shoes with great success. I remember my mother wearing them. Because they are so comfortable, I bought three pairs in beige, black and white.

Mea Sherim The old Jewish Quarters where old synagogues are being rebuilt. We tried to find out as much as we could about this fascinating city, but we had long delays driving around due to...Willie Brandt and entourage! We planted trees in the Kennedy Peace Forest; mine were dedicated to the memory of my dear parents. A trip to Bethlehem was also sandwiched in. The Arabs there are Christian and very friendly. As this was a quiet time for them business-wise, they were willing to give really good deals to us shoppers.

Guest Speakers at Our Dinners Moshe Kol, Minister of Tourism, and his wife spent the first Friday night with us, blessing the bread and wine. He has a very interesting background, was involved with Youth Alijah for nineteen years and was responsible for over 20,000 children, mostly orphans, reaching Israel. He was also connected with the Defense Department and is the author of numerous books. He urged us to take a message back to our chapters: Please come to Israel, as tourists or as new settlers; Israel needs you and, to be honest, also your money! He cited some of the adventures and experiences waiting for everyone. With the Bible in your hand, he said, you can visit the past and pray at the ancient wall and other sites. You can visit a kibbutz, swim in the Mediterranean or in the glittering Lake Kenereth and, to top it all off, climb Massadah. Great changes have occurred since 1967, he continued, and, if the Arabs want it, a great future awaits all of us. Sure, there are problems, but our streets are safe at any time of the day or night. Just come and enjoy!

The Minister went on to say that he was not at all happy with the Hadassah tourism development. Tourism currently consisted of fifty percent Jews, forty five percent Christian and five percent Arab. There were 250,000 Arabs who visited the country last year. He promised to encourage more tours like ours, at reduced prices, for the future. Mrs. Usdan informed us that a winter tour was in the planning for $599. Moshe Kol talked at length about Youth Alijah, one of his pet projects, and he mentioned with pride that one of the orphans he personally brought in, Eleaza, is now Chief of the Army. With a smile, he appointed all of us ambassadors and gave each of us a medal struck for the Twenty Fifth Anniversary of the State of Israel. He also invited questions. I asked why there were no tours leaving directly from the West Coast flying via El Al. He then explained that the FAA has to give permission for El Al to land, either in San Francisco or Los Angeles, before tours can be arranged via the pole to Lod Airport.

The next evening, we had a cocktail party attended by Mrs. Jacobsohn, former Hadassah president and Dr. Kalman Mann, Director General of Hadassah Medical Organization. Dr. Mann is a fifth-generation Israeli. He talked at length about the medical services and gave us some statistics: 23,000 patients per year are treated in 720 beds. Emergency rooms treat one million patients. Outpatients number five million. He sees the role of Hadassah as fourfold: imparting knowledge, creating knowledge via research, social services and community services.

Right now there are hundreds of research projects; papers

published by Hadassah Medical Teams are sent all over the world and are included in all reputable libraries. He called Israel a progressive modern country with superb health care, willing to share its knowledge with all the peoples of the world.

Mrs. Charlotte Jacobsohn thanked our illustrious guest and remarked that hearing him in person was so different than seeing him on television. She urged us to look upon this visit so as to give us a new perspective of Israel and to tell about it at home. She reminded us that the next years are of critical importance and the Jews of America must be made to realize this.

After a quiet Shabbath spent around the pool, we had to pack and get ready to leave Jerusalem. Due to the fact that we were divided into five groups, each of them now going in different directions, we also had been assigned different days to visit the Hadassah installations. Unfortunately, we were supposed to visit them all on one morning and then take the long drive via Jericho to Massadah. It was not good planning and it did not work out. First of all, our "villain" was in evidence again and traffic in Jerusalem was at a standstill, coming or going. When we finally reached the hospital at Ein-Keren, we were already late and had time for only a very short visit. We could devote to the Chagall windows less than four minutes! I had been in this hospital before as a visitor and was pleasantly surprised to see how much it had been enlarged and beautified. On to Mt. Scopus, again through stop-and-go traffic. Right now this complex is in the middle of construction. We climbed around cranes, stones and glanced into half-finished buildings, to me, a waste of time. Soon it will be an imposing site and just knowing that it is ours again made us happy. Next in line was the combined Seligsberg-Brandeis campus. An interesting school, but nearly impossible to find parking there, just like everywhere else in the world.

Finally we are on the road to Jericho. It was very hot driving to this oldest inhabited city in the Middle East. Once there, we found that we had a flat tire. Another long wait, but here at least we put the delay to good use. Our guide took us to recent archeological digs, which I personally found extremely interesting; most of the others could care less. On we went to a most interesting drive along the Dead Sea. What a desolated, but salty area. Yes, salt is the ingredient here. All along the beach are resorts. People come here to alleviate pains of arthritis and rheumatism as well as skin diseases. Oases like Ein Gedi attract lots of patients.

Our goal was the famous rock of Massadah, but we arrived five minutes after the cable car had closed down for the day. Big disappointment! Yet, while on the drive to our overnight hotel in Arad, our two stalwart Israelis came up with a brilliant idea. If we could get up at 4:30 AM the next morning, they would take us to the other side of the rock, only twelve miles from Arad and we would climb it via the Roman Pathway, thrown up by the Romans 2000 years ago to conquer Massadah. It is only a climb of fifteen to twenty minutes and not too steep. In fact, Israelis can climb it in eight minutes! Most of us decided right away to do it.

In Arad, a brand new city, we stayed at the Hotel Massadah. This town is located high above the Dead Sea, lovely, abreeze with fresh air, clean looking, it houses quite a few Russian immigrants or *Olims.* There are lots of baby carriages too as these towns attract the younger people. We were provided a good dinner and the rooms were small but adequate. We all met around the pool after dark to listen to an interesting speaker, Robert Gamis, a Canadian and former newspaper reporter who has settled here. He gave us some information on his town: 9,000 inhabitants now, but they are building for 15,000 by the year 1975. Big chemical outfits are close by, pot-ash and their like. He reported that most of the *Olims* have a hard time at the beginning because of the new language, different climate and trying to find jobs, but that they have the will and they do succeed; most of them seem to be happy.

Up at 4:30 AM, we were ready for our big adventure. On the way, we saw herds of camels, bedouins and their tents. We noticed at one place by the road that they were watering their goats and camels from a pipeline laid across the wasteland.

Our "nemesis" had one more surprise for us. Lo and behold, when we got close to Massadah, it seemed that the entire Israeli

Army was camped there, with a few policemen sprinkled in. Willie Brandt was coming! Which meant that we were forbidden to climb up. Well, at that our Itzhak and Mordechai girded for war. You should have heard the curses in Hebrew over the telephone...and then the talk grew loud and thunderous. No, no! Yes, yes! There was much shouting and gesticulating. In the end, they radioed Minister Moshe Kol in Jerusalem at 5:30 AM, asking for permission to advise the assorted high brass to let Hadassah go. And our Minister came through, thundering, "These people have a better right to climb Massadah than Willie Brandt will ever have!" Triumphantly, we started up, but halfway another officious officer wanted again to force us down. Nothing doing! We marched right around him and finally reached our goal, the top of Massadah. What a magnificient, overpowering site. Our guide, Itzhak, explained the history. Most of us knew the tragic story. Herod had built two palaces here in order to have a well-organized retreat, if needed. His best engineers and architects figured out a way to make life bearable in the Judean desert. Cisterns were dug to catch the twice-yearly heavy rainfall and marble floors and bathing pools were installed. But the palaces were never used and later on, bands of desperate Jews found refuge here. After the fall of Jerusalem, men, women and children lived here for years, hiding and enduring. During the bloody Bar Kochba Revolution (the last outbreak of Jewish nationalism), all of Palestine was laid to waste and finally the Romans beleaguered the fortress of Massadah, where about 900 people had sought refuge. The Romans built a pathway of sand and stones for their machines and soldiers after learning that there was no other way to take Massadah. After two years, when they finally made their last assault and reached the top, they made a grisly discovery. Over 900 men, women and children had chosen suicide or murder rather than become slaves. With reluctant admiration, the Romans accepted this fact. Only an old woman and some small children had hidden in a cave and later told their story to the famous renegade Jew, Josephus Flavius, who made this tale immortal. It was not believed until recent archeological discoveries proved every word.

Just imagine yourself on a high table-shelf mountain over-looking the grim Judean hills and the Dead Sea. In the clear desert air you can see for miles around. It is an impregnable fortress with cleverly built water cisterns, kitchens, baths, houses, palaces and two synagogues. One of the most astonishing finds were the Mikve's or ritual baths, which according to Orthodox Rabbis were built exactly to the law laid down in the Bible. The mosaic floor, heated tepariums (bath houses), all tells of splendor, desolation and an undying spirit. Massadah today has a deep meaning for all Israelis: *Never again* will we be homeless and slaughtered like cattle. For all of us, Massadah was an unforgettable moment in our lives.

On to Beersheba, a growing and noisy desert community, and Ashkalon, where we had lunch. Here an adventure befell me. After selecting from a kind of smorgasbord, I sat down and the chair collapsed, literally falling apart under me. I landed flat on my back on the floor, but luckily, I am very resilient and light-footed and nothing serious happened. I was shaken up and sore, as can be imagined, and kept very quiet the rest of that day. While in Ashkalon, we inspected the latest discovery, uncovered while digging a road: a beautiful marble sarcophagus, second century A.C.E., completely intact, exhibited in a glass case at a little roadside park.

Now on to Ashdod, a completely new city and harbor, built especially for the new oil pipeline.

We arrived in Tel-Aviv quite tired, late in the afternoon and checked into the Dan Hotel, located right on the beach. The changes here are even more evident than in Jerusalem. In ten years, the city has enveloped all its former suburbs, traffic is snarled up, highways have traffic jams, shops are over-crowded and pollution has arrived. As for swimming in the blue Mediterranean...oil slicks, tar and garbage are merrily floating around there at times. Notwithstanding, at 7:00 AM quite a few inhabitants are taking their morning swim and I went in too.

We visited the new Tel-Aviv University, modern with a lovely campus. Our guide explained to us that by the time a student gets his degree here, he is ready for the home next door, an old age home. Students start college when they are almost thirty years of age, due to the obligatory Army Service and the need to work a few years in order to accumulate the funds.

On to Rehhovoth and the Weizman Institute with its beautiful buildings and memorials in a park-like setting. Science and research buildings dot the landscape.

Jaffa, now an art colony, was our next stop and it was very pleasurable. We strolled around, had lunch and made purchases. There can be no doubt about it; Hadassah women love to shop and bargain and we must have raised the GNP of Israel quite a bit. Who can resist all that gorgeous jewlery, rings, earrings, chains, Yeminite handiworks and other enticing merchandise?

We also visited a hostel for the *Olims* and, as a special favor to Hadassah, we were permitted to question and to talk to a few of the newcomers. They come from South America, Lithuania, Russia and New York. They are helped with all of their problems, housing, shopping, language, etc., by the Jewish Agency which also tries to find jobs for them after their five months of training in the Hebrew language.

Tel-Aviv has 400,000 inhabitants and they all seem to meet on the main streets every afternoon. A most unusual moment for me occurred when I asked a German-speaking lady, who was chatting with a friend, for directions. We started to talk and she asked me where I was born. It turned out that she came from Kassel in Germany. When I mentioned that my husband was from there too and told her that his original name was Lewandowski, she immediately asked, "Is his first name Paul?" It turned out that she knew him and his family well! Isn't that unbelievable? When I told Paul about her, he remembered her very well and, as I have her address, he is going to write to her.

Early the next morning, we were off to the north along the coast via Herzliah, a lovely drive to Hadassah Neurim Rural Vocational Education Center, Emek Hefer and Kfar Vitkin, all beautifully situated on the Mediterranean. A Youth Alijah village, formerly a British Camp, opened in 1953. It is now an agricultural school for children from fourteen to eighteen years of age. Many Oriental children are there and only a few Arab children.

Out of 1,300 children, seventy-five percent are boys and sixty-five percent of the children live there. The curriculum is flexible. Forty percent of the cost is paid by Hadassah and sixty percent by the government. There are constant improvements being made. Just last year, central heating was installed. We were taken to hangers where young mechanics build airplanes from scratch, assemble radios and other electronic gadgets. They present classes in wood working, plumbing, etc. In other words, it is a fabulous place to send young American children and every Youth Alijah chairman should visit and see for herself. Roomy bungalows and a big athletic field are all part of it.

Rishon-Le Zion We visited a winery and an olive wood factory. Tiberias is situated on a beautiful lake where we had lunch. I spent three days there ten years ago and again I was struck by the beauty of this fresh water lake, the only one in Israel. Very good care is taken that the lake will not be polluted and secondary treatment plants are all around. The city has grown to almost triple the size it was in 1963. Near the famous hot springs, archeologists have uncovered the remains of a synagogue in astonishing condition. Beautiful mosaic floors, columns and adjoining Roman baths to take advantage of the hot springs were discovered.

Our visit and overnight stay at the Kibbutz Nof Ginosar was an outstanding one. The motel is run by the older members, which keeps them occupied and still contributing to the income of the kibbutz.

All this we learned from a slide presentation given by one of the elders at night. It was founded in 1934 by young Israelis, who graduated from the agricultural school of Ben Scheme and immigrants from Central Europe, mostly Germany and Austria, who knew nothing about the land. Their aim was to create a community based on productive self labor, collective responsibility, equality of status and opportunity for all.

Well known even in ancient times for its fertile soil and good climate, Nof Ginosar in 1934 sported only stones and sand without a tree or anything green within miles. In 1937, there were the first temporary dwellings with watchtower, required due to Arab attacks. Hard back-breaking work was needed in order to clear the land, start fisheries, plant crops, harvest and sell. Slowly the kibbutz grew with new members, more children; a primary school was established and later, a high school.

When the first Ginsar-born children reached adulthood, they went away for the military service, but all of them returned as full members and carried on. Today, 500 people live there, working in the rich plantations of banana, cotton, vegetables, fruits, dairy herds or in the ships, fishing on the lake. Vineyards, citrus groves, carp ponds, dot the park-like grounds and visitors from all over the world stop to see it. Willie Brandt was there the day before us.

A cultural center, which is part of it, was built in 1960. It contains a large library, dining hall, club and music rooms. All in all, it is astonishing what has been achieved here. One feels ashamed to think that all we could and can contribute to a state like Israel is money.

I got up before sunrise and strolled around taking pictures, watching the fishing trawlers coming in. It was so peaceful and, I am sure, I heard a nightingale singing.

Golan Heights One can only wonder at the courage of the young Israeli soldiers who captured these hills, fortifications and bunkers occupied by Syrian Arabs who were outfitted with the best weapons available. Under constant fire, they literally inched up towards the entrenched Syrian batteries, up vertical walls in order to free the settlers below from the constant fears under which they had lived for years. Nearly daily, the Arabs fired on them and killed with absolute immunity. Now, their turn had come, but almost 200 young Israeli soldiers had to give their lives before the Syrians retreated. Now that these heights belong to Israel, they will never be given up. New settlements come into being; the soil is rich volcanic earth where for thousands of years nothing grew but thistles and thorns. Stones are liberally sprinkled around, but there is underground water and once the land is cleared, almost anything can be grown here.

Safed We only spent a very short period of time in this charming hill-town. One synagogue and an art center was visited here, not enough to get acquainted with the history of this famous place.

Rosch Hanikra On the border between Israel and Lebanon, a cablecar takes you to the famous underwater caves, which reminded me very much of the Blue Grotto in Capri. Very interesting formations. None of us were couragous enough to enter Lebanon, but one manly soul put one foot across the borderline.

Haifa A beautifully situated city, reminding me of San Francisco. On to the Dan Carmel Hotel, which we all thought to be the best and most elegant hotel of our trip. It presented a gorgeous view with a half-moon bay and a green and white town spread out on different levels. For the plain pleasure of living, Haifa would be my favorite; also the climate and the beaches are much better than anywhere else in Israel. Of course, Jerusalem has more attractions and is historically more important. Quite close is the city of Accre, famous since ancient times and lately outstanding archeological finds have been made there. In order to show how one civilization builds its cities on top of an older one, they have cut into old Accre like into a chocolate layer cake. The top or youngest layer shows a Turkish floor; next down is the dining hall of a crusader castle, still in beautiful condition; even deeper, a Roman bath is shown and below that, a Greek mosaic floor can be admired. That is as far as tourists are allowed, as of now, but the archeologists are at work farther down to find a Phoenician layer and who knows what is below that? It makes one stop and think. So many civilizations have come and gone. What will be written about our time someday?

For the last two days, we were on our own: swimming, sunning, shopping, phoning old friends and maybe visiting. We were up early Sunday morning at 4:30 AM to catch our plane in Lod for the long flight home. There is a direct flight on a 747 El Al to New York (about fourteen hours), then again a three-hour wait before catching a United Airlines plane for Portland. After five hours, I arrived, tired but happy to be greeted by my dear husband, Paul; this at 8:30 PM on that same Sunday.

How can I sum up these fantastic fourteen days? I cannot. I have not even mentioned the concert and opera which I attended, the newspapers that I read telling about future cultural events and festivals, the bookstores and the lovely playgrounds, the hustle and bustle of commerce and the vibrant life on the streets; the ravishingly beautiful green countryside and, in contrast, the Judean desert, stark, yellow-white, burning; standing before the Wall and on top of Massadah... All of this combined spells: ISRAEL.

You've simply got to see for yourself.

> Edith R. Lavender
> Portland Chapter of Hadassah
> Theodor HERZL Group
> Vice President and Educational
> Chairman

Part VI
Mankind

Search

When first conceived, we seek to grow from a tiny seed into a living placenta, adhering to the womb which we call home. We partake in the very process of creation. Just as the force of Nature brought into being the Universe, we absorb into us the lifeblood encapsulated into the compartment of our body and soul, entrusted there from generation to generation by that very implantation.

We complete the cycle of our growing process, we are ejected, just like Adam and Eve from Paradise, to fend for ourselves, to search. We cry for food and find it in our mother's breast, that soft wing of heaven which we gently touch during the sucking process. But all too soon we are evicted again and must stand on our own two little feet, groping for ourselves. Our eyes open, we see a great big world which only yesterday did not know of our existence. Yet today, we act as if she is ours, feeling that we own her rather than she us. We stride upon her with possessive steps, heavier and firmer as we grow, yet continuing to search for food, for pleasure, for happiness.

While maturing, we learn to realize that we are but a pawn in the great chess game of Nature, used and moved according to her design, not ours. Even though we search for individuality, we are invariably forced into a pattern. We marry, finding a partner who, like we ourselves, is the product of the same process.

Are twenty years, sometimes less and often more, enough time to find our other half, that component which makes us whole? I think that the right partner is pre-destined. Even though Nature seems to be such a serious matter, in a playful way, she mixes humanity like a crossword puzzle, laughingly telling us: go and seek for your counterpart.

Sometimes we do find that partner and sometimes we don't.

TIME

Time ticks away
It masters all...
But Eternity it cannot sway

SNOW

Snow depicts life in its reverse stage.
It comes at evening and leaves at morn.

In Fall, when Nature goes to sleep,
Which may well be called a little death,
Snow furnishes a white blanket
With which to cover her.

When Spring comes, which is birth,
We look at snow as if it were a bridal veil
With which to cover the sweet young land
That suddenly presents itself in all its fertility.

Then there is just enough snow left
For children to play with,
To build an image of themselves,
Which will – just as they – fade away
At the proper time.

FAITH

Fear knocked at the door

Faith answered

No one was there

This inscription was lettered during the time of the battle of Dunkirk at the Hinds Head Hotel, Bay, England.

I STOOD AT THE OCEAN'S SHORE

I stood at the ocean's shore,
A little man perched near a vast expanse.

Planes flying in the air,
And boats floating on the wavy sea,
Both bearing witness to man's ingenuity.

A city borders all along,
Where people live, that wondrous breed,
Who can stretch an arm to heaven,
And wade in mud knee-deep.

All this is covered with the majesty of sky,
From which comes our strength and weakness,
The resolve by which to live and die.

I stood at the ocean's shore,
A little man perched near a vast expanse.

Life in the Raw – 1895

Remember the day when you left your father's house to go into the wide, wide world to become what is generally termed "a success?" With a satchel containing your toothbrush and visions of the future, you set out.

The first person you contact for a job in this land of plenty and freedom to work, tells you that you are much too young to be even considered for employment. The next prospective employer, a highly respected member in the community, spouts out in all sincerity that he wants to see recommendations.

Finally you find a friendly soul, a man who is willing to exploit you to the best of his abiliy. You start to work tomorrow morning punctually at 7:00 AM milking the cows, cleaning the stable (the one that Augeas owned seemed more like a sterilized hospital room in comparison) and then you go out to farm the land and suddenly, you have become a part of that famous backbone of our country, the farmer. Then you go back to feed the livestock and oh boy, were they living it up, squeezing the food down their throats like a tax collector squeezes his victim. Finally, dinner time comes, usually in the dark to save the kerosene, the moon shining free of charge outside. More often than not, your neighbors next to you, across the table and even from the far ends of it stick their forks into your hand trying to get their share and yours as those were the only shares available to the common man in those days. Early to bed and early to rise is the motto. Even the early bird was not safe then, lest one of us take the worm right out of his mouth.

Seven years have passed. You remember to read your Bible often and note the story of Jacob who got fooled more than once serving seven years. During those seven years, you dream of the big city, those slick city-folk, you have seen out at the farm, people who seem to have everything without ever having to lift a finger. So, you quit and holler, "City, here I come!"

By golly, before long someone takes pity on you and gives you a job as a janitor. This time, you are smart. You watch the fellow directly ahead of you and soon you are asked to replace him because you told the boss that you would do the work for less than the other guy and such an offer the boss could not resist. That way, you work yourself up from job to job, just like a man climbs a ladder. Sometimes, the going is rather slippery and you have to hold on tight with both hands, but you make it.

Your business is your own and other people are working for you now. However, for every dollar you earn, you seem to need twice as much. The more you make, the less you seem to have left. Suddenly relatives, who for years did not remember your name, seem to have taken a refresher course and have learned how to stretch out a hand effectively. The one achievement you had set as your life's goal, that one dream which kept you going during all those many years, was to become financially independent and now you are... and you are not.

On the way, you acquire a wife, children, a home. You have days off now, days of leisure, looking at your neighbors on the left and on the right, in the back and across the street, you see them working like beavers, painting their houses, patching the roofs, digging up their gardens. This gives you a feeling of guilt. Thus, you decide to do your part in the peace effort. You gather your energy and mow your lawn yourself. After the lawn, the roses need your attention, the nasturtiums, the azaleas, the lilacs. Then there are the weeds; one plural does not suffice to describe their multiplicity. You are dead tired and you think that you are finished... and finished you are. Laura needs to be chauffeured to her ballet lessons, Richard to be transported to the Boy Scout meeting, Carla must be picked up from the hair dresser and your wife wants you to take her to the grocery store for the weekly shopping.

You read a book entitled *How To Live Longer* and there it states, "To ensure a longer life, lots of rest and relaxation are required." Therefore you start to take it easy. You go to the office late and come home early. Gradually every member of the family considers you a loafer and friends call you a good-for-nothing. Right or wrong, there is no right. All your life you have toyed with the idea of retiring early, to make a leisurely trip around the world with your wife. The statistics say that these are the prospects: If you have the money, nine chances out of ten, you won't live to do so; if you live, your wife probably passes on before you or if you are both living and healthy, you can be sure the necessary money was lost in the depression which just happened to hit; if you have your wife, your health, your money, your life…it is very questionable that the world will still be there for you to see. Therefore, the most sensible thing for you to do is to disappear.

From the Chair of Honor in Heaven reserved for you to compensate for the complete mess you made of your life, you observe what's going on beneath you on the good old earth.

There you see your grandson, that rascal, squander the money you so unselfishly accumulated. Every time you had the urge to spend a couple of bucks during your journey down there, you refrained from doing so because you wanted to amass a fortune for your family. "What a fool I have been," you say to yourself, "I should have lived it up and my grandson would appreciate me more. The only concern he seems to have is to experience the most fun possible and to let his children fend for themselves."

When most of the money is gone, your grandson starts a movement of social reform, he who has never done a lick of work in his life. "What is wrong with the world," he says self-righteously, "is that money can be inherited. Each person should create his own pile. If a person wants to live well, let that man work harder; if a person is happy with very little, no reason why that man should not loaf. To do away with the unpleasant task of paying taxes, why not just leave the principal to the state when you die, rather than hasten death by that yearly agony. If there is a widow, let the state support her."

"A fine seed I planted there," you say to yourself.

Thirty years later, you happen to take another glance down there. By golly! What has happened? A mass of happy people float around yonder. Your grandson's ideas have become the norm of the day. No more pampered grandsons in positions which they have not earned. The ambitious and able ones are the leaders and the others let themselves be carried along. Bank vaults are empty because people help their fellowman. Instead of wasting time accumulating money, people utilize it to learn about the history of man, his trials and tribulations. They look at paintings again from which the dust of centuries has been removed. Culture experiences a rebirth. Poverty has disappeared because it is illegal.

Did I say that my grandson was a rascal? I made a grave error. A grandson of mine could only be a *great* man.

Old Souls for Sale

Have you ever shaken hands with yourself? This might sound preposterous; yet, it is time that you learn to do it. Get acquainted with the stranger who lives within you, your other you. Professor Sigmund Freud (long since passed on) recognized the existence of the subconscious mind and in his scientific writings laid the foundation to what is known to us as Psychoanalysis.

When we speak of a good and evil soul within us, we actually are talking about the conscious and subconscious mind within ourselves. Every single thought which comes to us is the result of who became the winner in the battle of these two minds. When you say to yourself early in the morning, "Should I get up or stay in bed five minutes longer?", whatever you are going to do depends on the outcome of this verbal battle. Society teaches us that having learned to get up right away (in other words, your ability not to succumb to that five-minute urge) is when you are well on the way to become a successful member of it. Were we still citizens of the State of Paradise, your action would definitely be frowned upon. So you see, right from the start, that your decisions depend largely on the state of mind in which you are living. Basically both of our minds have not the slightest idea of good or bad, right or wrong. Our parents implanted these ideas there when first they wiggled their finger at us saying, "Hm, hm, don't do that!" It would have been so nice to stay living uncensored for the rest of our lives, so comfortable, so at ease.

The science of hypnosis, which means putting the conscious mind to sleep while awakening the subconscious mind in its place, states that you first must learn complete relaxation, both physically and mentally. Recognize tension and drop it. Smooth out your brow, relax the neck muscles by dropping your head forward, sag your shoulders, breathe slowly, let your feet dangle and your hands rest comfortably on your thighs. Now add mental relaxation. Think of pleasant occurances. Become an escapist, which by no means is a crime. It definitely makes you live happier and longer. It makes you see, hear and think better. Tests have been made and proof established along these lines. Aches and pains, mental or physical, can be hypnotized away. The cause of the physical pain will not disappear, but this method aids in keeping the patient calm until the doctor can diagnose the illness. Mental aches, you can easily cure by learning how to put yourself in the proper frame of mind. Many people get confused with the right timing of when to use which of the two minds. Have you ever noticed when the conscious mind of your fellow workers seems to be asleep, especially after you ask them to do something? Say the words, "coffee break," and notice how they immediately become wide awake. It is really remarkable how they can relax!

The use of hypnosis is of particular value in putting our finger on the cause of mental ills. If somebody is moody, we don't blame him or her, but put the responsibility fairly and squarely upon the parents. We immediately assume that his father once spanked this character too hard. But when? Difficult problem? Not at all. The subject is put into hypnotic sleep using the method of regression, which means going back into the life of the person to find the cause of it all. The human mind is just like a long-playing record; we can set the needle back to any point, even to the early years of a person's life. When we reach childhood, the subject may act and talk childishly and tell us exactly what happened on a certain day. Eventually, we hit the right spot which tells us what it is that bothers this individual. We release the subject from his mental burden by telling the subconscious mind to forget it, wipe the matter from the mind and the individual then becomes a happy, normal person again. You see, the subconscious mind knows more about us then we do ourselves (meaning our conscious mind). I have often thought if it might not be beneficial to humanity were we to learn how to turn ourselves inside out, making the subconscious mind our conscious living and putting the conscious mind to sleep. So very little would be lost. Stupidity and ignorance would be no more.

Don't think for a moment that we would stop with the first

year of life. That would be much too simple for man. The improbable, we do today, the impossible, tomorrow. Not only are we attempting to reach other planets, we are also reaching back in time, wanting to put our finger on old souls. You must have read about the case of Bridey Murphy, which proves that point in question. Here, a woman was regressed under hypnosis beyond day one and was able to recall places, actions and names of people who lived long before her time somewhere in England. Investigations (which means prowling through old records) proved that these people lived at a time several hundred years prior. What does this prove? Nothing is more simple than that: the soul which lives within us is a used soul, sort of a secondhand affair, when it was given to us at birth. We all know that the body dies at death, but not the soul. Oh no, *that* lives on. Now what is this body-less soul to do? Fly aimlessly around? This would create a traffic jam pretty soon. To solve this difficult problem of the highways on the skyways, every newborn baby is supplied with one of these souls. Once in a while, when there is a greater supply than demand (with birth control and all) a sign goes up: Old Souls For Sale. This explains why some people think that they are Napoleon, wives believe that their name is Rockefeller and in many people, two souls seem to find a housing place. That is when you discover a side of yourself you never knew was there.

You might think of another person, "What a louse." There you have it in a nutshell; that is where his soul came from. I, the writer, (yes, I am still sound and sane and with you and with all my souls) have the distinct feeling that the soul of Socrates was implanted within me. When I showed the outline of this book to the publisher recently, he handed me a cup of poison.

So you think that you know yourself? Bah!

Put yourself in self-hypnotic sleep and get acquainted. You might be surprised at what a charming character your subconscious mind actually is and how easy and pleasant it is to live with him. Nothing wrong with letting him do all the heavy lifting, mentally and physically, while you sit back and relax.

It is about time that you shake hands with yourself!

AWAKENING

Spring, you source of Youth,
You are here again,
Filling the countryside with color and freshness,
Putting the beginning to an eternal cycle,
Life-giving with scent, budding, sprouting.

Do not let us think of growing, maturing,
Which are not of your making.
Let the eye, the mind stay right here,
Not hurdle the mountain,
Nor delve into what lies beyond.

Let us believe that life is arrested here,
That Nature, Beauty, those rare deportments
Will never change their attire,
Shall remain just as my mental eye sees them.

The first awakening, the first greeting,
The first smile, the first laughter,
Let them be last as they are first,
Every single day, always,
And Eternal Youth will be ours.

Confusion

It is said that nearly five billion people presently inhabit this earth. How many have trod it since the beginning of time no one has undertaken to figure out, as of yet. Only the national debt could in all probability surpass that astronomical figure.

Imagine that many lives and yet each one lived in isolation, each one with its only personal dream, may this dream be in the head of a fellow savage or the idea of the Theory of Relativity coming from the head of an Albert Einstein. Singly, each one of us arrived alone. Even a quintuplet must be slapped singly upon his behind to start breathing, to switch itself in on the juice of life which flows so freely for all, humans and beasts.

Unrefutably, the animal world presents itself in so much more beautiful a dress, a mixture of color surpassed only by the rainbow, not just white, black or yellow, as in the human race.

I don't know what ideas are in the head of a sand flea or an elephant, nor can I tell for sure what is in the head of a human being, but I will try to analyze it for you. Wiser men before me have made an effort to tell us, but as Adam said to Eve, we must try and try again. Everyone after them must have said this to each other as well as the population explosion of today proves, they are still trying.

No matter what, each one of us beings will stand alone, must fend for himself, in trying to find the purpose of it all: why we are here, what to do with our time and how to stretch it like a rubberband without breaking it.

Communication, though a long word, is the short of it. We do it in speech, in writing, in order to break down the barriers of loneliness. Thus the institution of the family was born, for a man and a woman pledging themselves to care for the young. From that first moral fibre developed the clan, the community, the city, the state, the federal government and with that, those wonderful tax systems that each one has put in place. The copies of those tax returns are the certificates which we should frame as an honorary degree of "Doctor of Man" and hang it above our beds, so that we can fall asleep easier with this high-est of all citations lulling us to sleep.

Still we are far from our goal. The clans are still in existence, races and religions still look at each other as inferiors, nations still do not trust each other and we spend a great deal of our national funds to build sophisticated weapons which neither country plans to use. Maybe we got so accustomed to building arms that we do not remember why because it would destroy the arms industry, an important segment of our national pro-ductive output.

We must learn from the ocean that only in unity lies strength. Were each drop of water to fend for itself, no mighty ocean would exist. Were each ray of sun to shine alone, darkness only would encircle the globe.

A drip will become a drop, a mighty ocean of enlightenment.

LIFE WHAT ART THOU?

An expression, a gesture
Of the instinctive desire
To fulfill oneself.
A chase, like the hunter's,
To reach a goal set,
To put the final touch
Upon one's ambition, endeavor.
Oh, to love something, someone,
Beyond our physical and psychic capabilities,
To outdo, outreach ourselves into posterity, infinity.

To state: I have added
An infinitessimal iota
To this world
To make it a better one.
To see, to hear, to smell, to touch,
Since in unison they enable us to emote,
To try to understand the glory
Of the heavens and the earth
And make us sing of the wonders of the world.
To lust for life, that is what thou art...
Life

Lonely Only

It is said that we are all born equal, which means that we are ejected in equal fashion, but at that moment, equality ends. Each one of us is endowed with different qualities, raised in various economic stratas. Some of us are born into Western civilization, Eastern or Third World countries. There, to say the least, the scope of development is curtailed from the start and equalization ends.

Basic developments given to us are hunger, thirst and the deep need for being loved. Civilized parents know that someday we have to fend for ourselves. Therefore, they try very hard to instill us with knowledge. Unfortunately, with it they teach us prejudice, certainly not a God-given feeling, and hate, which is neither. Were we to live, theoretically speaking, in paradise, maybe love would get the upper hand and falsehood would never enter our minds. Being aware of that, we would not even have to burden ourselves with the ceremony of marriage, which has been invented to protect the partners and their offsprings; divorce, needless to say, would not exist. After all, paradise prevails.

Need I tell you that this is not the case down here on earth. Survival is the motto; even though it is never mentioned, it screams from all the rooftops. How can you survive if kindness and love are all that you have to offer? Life is a battle. You have to matriculate from school, from college, whatever. Assume that you have jumped over all of these hurdles and have kept your health and your wits about you. The next step is to knock on the door of opportunity. Will it open? By hook or by crook (you probably will remember which one prevailed) you become what is so beautifully called "gainfully employed." By luck, the last depression did not divest you from your lifetime savings and you can indeed look forward to your golden years. (Does that expression come from the golden watch your boss will give you when you retire?)

The time has come. You are not only retired, but also tired to boot. You help around the house, play golf, entertain the grandchildren and you wonder what it was all about.

Lonely only.

Vacations

As the name implies, a vacation is vacating our present cubbyhole for another one; this, however, only for a short period of time. The feeling of earthlessness comes when we sit so very comfortably in a plane, which will carry us to the place of dreamed fulfillment. Flying like a Persian prince through the air, (maybe not on a Persian rug, but the equivalent of the red carpet service), loosens all feelings and burdens are conveniently dropped down to the forest over which we just happened to fly.

What else is there to do while comfortably seated in the plane but to project something we are destined to do all our lives? We try to predict the result of a test in school, ponder the relationship with a friend, weigh the consequences of a planned marriage, maybe a business venture in progress.

Soon we get there and again we plan. What are we going to do? Walk on the beach? Visit churches, cathedrals? No doubt we are going to visit museums, tire our feet and look forward to frequenting a deli nearby. Oh yes, we want to add to our font of knowledge and be able to say that we have been there too when someone proudly speaks of their travel experiences.

Vacation is the time to which people with imagination look forward from year to year. Vacation means getting away, changing of schedule, freeing oneself from the monotony of making and providing a living. Actually, the term, "living" is much too generous a word to describe that activity since living to me is an inspired activity, much more than working, eating, sleeping and looking at television. These are basic needs and the term, "I am providing a vegetation," would be so much more appropriate.

Vacation, mentally, is like changing from a work-a-day suit into the best-of-Sunday suit, giving a clean proud feeling, a sensation of worth. For once, spending money is not a matter of necessity, but of free will, wanting to get away, wanting to live a little. You stay in a fine hotel and try to use all their facilities, particularly the swimming pool where your children meet other kids. They have no problem meeting people. They do not analyze people like you do: from what fabulous city might they have come, what big position must that fellow over there with that attractive wife hold? Somehow you manage to talk to them and you find out that their circumstances are not much different from yours and that the magic city where you assumed they live is actually your own home town.

Just because vacationing is living, it also proves to be a strenuous process in trying to visualize the events of every coming day. Even the car seems to be jumpy. No wonder with all that excess baggage in the trunk! Everything is back there, but a sweater and a raincoat. Who thinks of coolness in summer or rain when our vacation can only be blessed by good weather? Rain is for others. Who can believe that the car needed a vacation long before we did; that, without hesitation, it can go dead between here and nowhere. Nothing can be deader than a dead car. That monster just sits there and gives you no indication what ails it. Somewhere at the gas station, they give it a kick in the right direction and there it coughs again. Though late, we reach our destination without having to starve or freeze to death on the way.

Time is such a pliable material. It lies there like a baby in its crib. It wants to be molded and it is up to us to adorn it, to make it festive. When a good time is had, it is we who fashioned it that way, not time itself. Time is remarkable because it is so rare, so unique. Don't ever take it for granted.

Aren't we lucky to do all this? We are healthy enough and most of all, have the finances to make travel possible. The fate of people who sleep under bridges comes to mind. Granted, we worked for it and worked hard at that. One terrible mis-adventure and we would have had to share their lot. Contemporaries might be able to save our soul, but if the minuses reached the upper hand, poverty is the only other alternative. There is no escape hatch for failure.

Vacation is more than travel. It also clears out the crevices of our minds so that we can start anew accumulating time, funds and ideas. A job is mechanical; it runs off according to a certain pattern. Vacations are different, touching the sense of curiosity, tingling the nerve of newness. Granted, we come home exhausted, in need of a rest from a splendid vacation. Yet... vacation, anyone?

Avocation

Often I have wondered which would have been the most gratifying life's work for me, had I, in addition to inclination, also the ability and training. I conclude that the role of an orchestra conductor would have been my choice.

A conductor controls down to his little finger elements which reach elevations closest to those the Almighty must have felt when he created the universe. The downbeat for the Earth and the upbeat for the Heavens...spherical music which, I am sure, accompanied the birth pangs of Creation itself.

An orchestra, a group of people, creates music by activating various instruments. Hands, chins, lips, feet, ears, eyes and, not least, the mind play an important role in this process.

Is the work of a conductor creative? When we go into a concert hall half an hour after the performance, none of the creative spirit which had prevailed there can be detected. That spirit has moved on.

Yes, the conductor is the complete master. He serves as a nerve center from which emerge the impulses of rhythm, modulation and co-ordination translated into musical expression. Composer and conductor are husband and wife, creating and recreating, kindling and inspiring the flame of interpretation and imagination.

Music is an international language, understood by all who can hear and yet interpreted differently by each human being. As it has inspired many to die in battle, it could and should inspire all of us to live in peace.

The Eternal Idol

It was a spring morning, more beautiful in its quietness and majesty than any other dawn. The birds were chirping away while fog rose from the valley like a veil from a virgin bride. The various shades of green represented a color play of boundless variation. All this was glorified by a spotless blue sky, engulfing that unforgettable touch of peace, youth and joy.

With the appearance of people in the fields, cars on the highways, trains on the circling band of rails, the young morn and its atmosphere seemed to be frightened away. A hissing wind came up, probably as an answer to man's challenge and heaven's bright face turned into serious gloom. That horizon, which had seemed to be such a protective cover, now looked more like a cracked ceiling, threatening to break at any moment. Then the mournful face dissolved into tears, the soft strokes of the wind turned into passionate blows, whipping up the dormant world into an exciting game of life.

Even though I was soaked to the skin, rain seemed to be nectar to my pores. Louder than ever, I sang my spring monologue into the air which seemed to harmonize through unseen organ pipes. The steady forward tread of my strong young body provided the rhythm. My mind was as light and as unburdened as an empty shell. Forward...that is all that I knew.

The going was getting rough. Frightened animals raced in front of me. Streams of water encircled me and trees broke under an unseen load. Was this the end, the penalty for having lived through the peaceful awakening of a new day?

Yet, I was firm in the belief that, beyond all of this, something equal to what I had just lost must be in wait for me. I had discovered years ago that the brightness of stars, the clearness of rain-washed stone, the beauty of reflection can be achieved only by a rough cruel process. I had learned that achievements in life were made possible only through suffering. The knowledge was planted within me that there can be no fulfillment of our innermost yearnings if we shirk or circumvent the bumps and mud puddles in the road of life.

Soon all this was swept away as fast as it had appeared. Nothing seemed real about the storm after it was gone. In front of my eyes, a picture was revealed like a Fata Morgana in the desert sun.

There she was, the idol of eternal youth, she of my dreams, the untouchable, the flame of beauty, the crystal of mind, more charming than I ever had imagined. There she stood, her light hair waving in the morning breeze, her dark eyes piercing, her smile embracing me.

When I stepped forward to seal this with just one kiss... emptiness was all that met my lips.

The Vacuum

We seem to hear, but not to understand. We see, but don't observe. We feel, but don't react.

Somewhere along the line, wave and wave length seem to be at a divergence. Two bodies can unite, but they cannot become one. Two souls can find a common denominator, but their thoughts will not be the same. We congregate, meditate; we become exalted; we try to understand; yet we cannot achieve fully. The battle between right and wrong can never be won by either side, since nobody really knows what is right and what is wrong. That is why two opponents can neither be entirely right, nor entirely wrong. Aspect alone will make the difference in a decision.

War, the most hideous of human inventions, can never be outlawed. The only alternative is to work on the elimination of the causes which most frequently have brought about war.

I, for one, believe that wars are based on maladjusted economics. Yet, no war has ever been fought in the name of economics. False pretenses, like religion and racial differences, are used as a smoke screen. Hitler accused the Jews, Stalin, the Capitalists (a religious sect which worships the god of finance). Yet, there is no communistic government that does not have the capitalistic ideology incorporated into its very acts; they just give it a different name. There is no capitalistic system that does not have a spark of feeling for the commune.

Life is a continuous tangle with all of these problems, none of which will ever be fully solved unless, someday, a ray of atomic or other energy succeeds in penetrating into that part of the mind where the basis for full and complete understanding still lies dormant.

The World's Flower Garden

What a varied garden do women in this colorful world present! What a visual feast to observe the beautiful blossoms gathered here. Dark and fiery ones which easily could have originated in Italy or Spain; light and breezy ones, probably from Sweden or Germany; vivacious and charming ones, shaded with copper, most likely from Poland or Hungary. Each flower has a character, a beauty and aroma of its own, exhaling the fragrance of individuality, sacrificing beauty to the span of its all-too-short life. Just to be, to display the character which makes each blossom unique, to fulfill the circular purpose for which God created each of them, to be a link, soft, yet iron-strong in the chain of creation.

Vain would be the flower's beauty were it not to entice the bee!

Life's fire, neatly laid in the housing of our bodies, needs just a spark to put it to flame. Some fires are slow to start; some ignite quickly and fizzle equally fast; some burn slowly, fiery red hot, linger on and only extinguish with life itself.

To see, to hear, to feel, to smell, to express, to give, to take... all this is part of the most complete vibration of our very being. Yes, it is the purpose of this most wondrous life in God's enchanting garden.

Mexican Mixture

Mexico – south of the border – just follow the jet and, better yet, have a seat on it.

From the moment you arrive in Mexico City, you are made participant in the hustle of that teaming city, a contradiction in every stone put upon the other, in every shout and action which ejaculates from these dark-skinned yet light-hearted people. How poor is poor? How well is well-being? Religion, it seems, has become the antidote to the poison of poverty which seems to have wrecked the bodies of the majority of the Mexican people. Oh, how enthralled they are when walking on their knees, thus slowly approaching the shrine, the church, the haven of their souls. Yet how wild they can become when attending the bullfight.

How welcome is the *coup de gras* which a bull receives after having been molested, kidded, outnumbered. I could see and feel so well what was going on in the bull's mind after he was chased into the arena and gawked at by the throng of thousands of people. What am I doing here? What do they want from me? Am I a Jew, a Black, that I must be hunted, speared? Why do they put that red carpet in front of my eyes when they know so well that I cannot stand that color? What are they doing to me, darn it! Another pair of spears into my neck? How beastly can a human being get? If they would only leave me alone! I am a pacifist by nature, like to chew the bull with other bulls; those of my kind like to be left alone. Isn't there an exit someplace to leave this arena of human disgrace, to go into a corner of my bullpen and lick my wounds? There is that darn *toreador* again and those beasts out there screaming, *"Ole! Ole!"* (whatever that means). Why do I have to be the innocent victim? Why am I the center of it all? Why was I born a bull? What chance do I have, a lonely animal against six of them with their swords and I with my poor eyesight and only two little horns on top of my head as weapons of defense? I feel my strength sapping. What have I done to deserve this? Had I been a sister to my brother or a devout Catholic, maybe I could have been saved all this. Come on, you heroes, you know that I can hardly stand on my legs anymore... let me have it and you can be so proud to have killed me, an innocent victim of man's brutality. Come on, *toreador,* man of the hour, great hero who now stands before me alone, applauded by all for killing a half-dead animal. Come on, let me have it! Oh, thank you so very much! *Gracias!*

How different Mexico reflects itself from a sun porch in Taxco, a sleepy village apparently unawakened by the passage of time. The clatter upon the cobblestones competes with the ringing of the church bells, begging the faithful to come to worship. Now and then a rooster proclaims mastery over his kingdom of hens with his *kikeriki.* All seems so peaceful, so untouched by the prolific tendencies of our time.

Mexico could well be called Mixeco, contrast upon contrast. Nowhere in the entire world can you find so exquisite a Museum of Anthropology as in Mexico City where the history of Mexico from its earliest beginnings, step by step, gives witness.

EXPECTATIONS

The lingering of the air before a storm,

The last command given by the general before the battle,

A child's closing of the eyes before the awakening to a birthday,

The cat perched to make the final jump in catching a bird,

A mother looking forward to the birth of her first child,

The conductor raising his baton to start the musicale,

Lovers cuddled in each others arms,

The dog begging for food with a hungry eye,

The political campaigner the night before the election:

Expecting, looking forward if for nothing else but

To see you.

Hm

Is there a more expressive word in the human dictionary than "Hm?" This sound is so fascinating because it conveys such a variety of moods. It could make an excellent title for a book, one which might even turn out to be a best seller with everyone interpreting the title in a somewhat different way, but all of them looking forward to an interesting epistle.

There is that "Hm," short, exhaled with an air of arrogance, the one that Walter Winchell made so famous in his reporting. "The meeting of the foreign ministers in Geneva will pave the way to peace. Hm." or "It is reported that the Arabs will treat the Jews in Israel like brothers. Hm." "How to make a million dollars on a thousand dollar investment. Hm."

Writings by H.L. Mencken, that great cynic of our time, may bring about such exclamatory noise. Irony, sarcasm, disbelief... no other sound can convey this meaning so very well.

"Hm?" with a question mark attached is another matter indeed. Like this: "Honey, you won't mind taking out the dog for his nightly walk, hm?" (It is 3:00 AM and fresh snow covers the ground.) How can you say no with a "hm" put before you, elongated, sweet, as if it were played on a harp? You simply cannot. "Oh, I would so love to go dancing tonight, Henry." (She pronounces Henry the French way for effect.) "Hm?" This after coming home from the office dead tired, having dreamt so longingly all day of a leisurely evening at home, the pipe at your side and the slippers on your feet. "Gladly, honey." "Let's visit Mother; she is such a lonely woman, hm?" You wish she were alone in Timbuktu among African Headhunters. Every time you visit her, she lets you know in a very subtle way that her daughter could have done so much better with someone else twenty-five years ago. "Oh, I would so like to have a new car, Sweetie, hm?" (Double sweet, double elongated; you simply have got to create it in its correct undertone to get the full impact.) Just yesterday you were trying to figure out on the back of a used envelope (who can afford a fresh new piece of paper?) how to affect your monthly payment on the car you traded in for the present one just a year ago. "Certainly, honey."

Hm, hm (staccato). Nobody can pronounce these sounds more convincingly than a child. "Will you leave the TV set and go to bed now?" Mother screams at the top of her voice. "Hm, hm!" This means in conversational English: Absolutely, positively no! Jump in the lake twice and come up once! Stand on your head all day long and I still won't do it! This, it seems, is the only weapon a child has in defiance. He cannot take the weekly allowance away from you; he cannot tell you to stay in your room all day and he cannot take a belt and show you. The child can, however, say, "hm, hm!"

Who does not want to throw away the yoke which binds? The child, the yoke of being educated; the father (who knows), the yoke of having to go to work every single day. But...one can't; life does not work that way. Had the parent not only threatened, but actually used that belt more often, this speech defect could have been easily cured; but then we parents consider ourselves civilized people and, in that capacity, we simply cannot do it.

Hm, hm, hm, hm. Four sounds, the first one long and the three following ones progressively shorter. This is the expression of, "Why on earth do I have to get up in the morning?" "When, by Jove, will there be an end to all that?" "For crying out loud... what next?" All of us have felt like this at times and were we to follow our inclination immediately "to make a splash on Broadway," this world would be depopulated and Broadway, indeed, not broad enough. Luckily, we get over these moods rapidly. Often we fall from one extreme into another. Soon, after someone compliments you on how pretty you look today, you are ready to go on a kissing spree just to let everyone know what a wonderful place this Mother Earth really is.

The most uninhibited, most natural sounds are the following: "Hm, hm..." long and expressive, speaking of culinary satisfaction. Being in the process of eating a piece of strawberry cake with plenty of whipped cream on top, "hm, hm..." It is permissable, according to Elsa Maxwell, to accompany these tones with a sound of smacking the lips, serving as exclamation marks.

There is an expression of feeling by two equally long-drawn exhalations, forced from the back of the throat about an octave lower in tone, "hm, hm," painful, mournful. The most exhilarant feelings in life are born of anguish, torment, agony. Were these elements non-existing, joy, exaltation, rapture too, would be unknown. When we want to give feeling to boundless happiness, the sound which we then ejaculate is exactly the same which we use when in pain. The pain of bringing forth and the joy of having brought forth. Tears too are born that way, giving relief. No two sounds express more deeply, more clearly that life is a cycle of motions and emotions.

"Hm hm…" that long drawn-out "hm" with a short one following. That is the one expressed with a shrug of the shoulders, a wrinkling of the forehead, the raising of the hand to form a question mark. "I just don't know what to make of it?" "Who can tell what the results will be?" "Will the world ever be a better place to live in?" This is the philosophical "hm, hm," a weighty question to which there is no answer. It gives so much stature to the questioner without having to indulge into the burden of responsibility of having to answer it.

"Hm, hm." This is the long, long expression with a melodic tail, about an octave higher in tone. "You don't say?" (half questioning, half repudiating.) Someone says to you, "The hat you are wearing today is simply atrocious." "Hm, hm?" Did I hear right? Did she really say what I think she said? Come again! In that split-second of time in which that tail is attached, the entire scale of human emotional register is played. Should the attacker refuse to waver, maybe even has the nerve to repeat that statement, the end result will be disastrous. It is like putting a dagger deep into the heart of the attacked and no such melodic sound will come forth again.

This completes the literary eruption which, when set to music, could well be called, "A Minor Variation on the Tone Play, Hm, Hm." All of these sounds which, at superficial absorbtion are without rhyme or reason, actually are deep-meaning words, words which should find a place in the dictionary and encyclopedia. They might be spelled the same, but

133

they are by no means voiced the same. They spell an entirely different meaning.

Which word has a deeper significance: Hm or antidisestablishmentarionism? The shortest or the longest word?

Hm?

Musings

Fools, fools we are – when clowns we could be.

* * *

The greatest mockery is voting every two years. What it really boils down to is legitimate theatre. Actors learn roles and deliver propaganda speeches which someone else has written and we, the voters, believe them to be their own brainchild.

* * *

The dictionary defines "politics" as: unscrupulous, crafty, artfully contrived. No wonder that we call politicians by that name. Any man who has to accept contributions in any shape or form becomes a slave before he can become a master.

* * *

When you finally retire after thirty years of service, the boss presents you with a golden pocketwatch, beautifully engraved with your name so it cannot be taken to the nearest pawnshop for ready cash. The first time in your life you have absolutely no reason to watch the clock, you are made the owner of one. You retire only to find that work was never as miserable as the millions of chores your wife finds for you to do. That's life. Yes, Sir.

* * *

Were the earth a paradise this side of heaven, words like "freedom" and "liberty" would never have entered our vocabulary. Disagreement, persecution and fear would not be part of our heritage.

* * *

Books are written and writers concoct fixations of their mind, put a title to it and it becomes "literature." It is either fictional or fact, even though it is probably impossible to invent a saga without interweaving biographical notes and a biography without fantasizing.

The bed is the beginning of everything, thus let us start there. I never asked my parents how I came about and furthermore, that would probably have been most embarrassing to do. I imagine that my father would have told me that he was in a romantic mood and you can figure out the rest for yourself. Anyhow, I am here and by all means a romantic.

* * *

When we read a book, we do it for many different reasons. A schoolboy or girl has to read; it is their assignment. A college student has to do it for a similar reason. He wants to get that shingle which in so many words says, "I am a doctor" or "you are a lawyer." Once you have it, how much easier life becomes. You can charge a horrendous sum of money for your knowledge, while any other slob has to be satisfied with minimum wage or thereabouts. Other people read because they are bored or they have too much free time on their hands; some want to learn, to be entertained or amused. Paperbacks generally have a very inviting cover accompanying a usually dull story.

* * *

Caring. We all care, if not only for ourselves and our family, for our friends and many people down the line, this through organizations, which make it their business to help. Where does one begin and where does one stop? Every day the need seems to become greater and just because you supported a cause once, you are expected to support it for the rest of your life. Your sensitivity to misery is exploited by putting you on the sucker list and organizations you never even heard of are suddenly sending you their wish list.

* * *

You might think that Inflation is something fairly new. We already had that dubious distinction in Germany in the 1920's. At that time, it happened that Germany switched one billion Marks into one Deutschmark, a new tender of money. In other words, the old money was not worth the paper the legal tender was printed on. Fortunes were lost overnight. That is the foundation that Hitler found in Germany and since you cannot establish a new movement without a scapegoat, he blamed the Jews. Somebody asked then, "Why not the bicycle riders?" The answer is, "Why the Jews?" Either group had as little to do with the problem as the other, but, as history has proven, marching, screaming, accusing, persecuting brings the desired results. In the old days, population explosions were controlled by pestilence and war. Now we do it by murder, insurrections and wars by any other name.

* * *

Where am I? Who am I? Why am I? At a superficial glance, these questions are three of thousands that beset us every day; questions, however, to which there is no answer. Analyzing them, we must conclude that they would be the first to be asked by a newborn baby had he or she the mental capacity to do so. Where am I? Who am I? Why am I? How did I get here on this planet, awakened from deep slumber of the No-Where, simply having been thrust, tossed by an unseen, forever-moving force? I find myself waking, working, wandering in a repetitious circle, seemingly under my own power and yet so obviously attached to an unseen string, manipulated by such deft hands, just like a marionette. Why am I surrounded by my contemporaries? By a designed plan or simply by the fall of a pair of dice? Who is the person beside me whom I love, pretend to know? Can anyone, no matter how closely scrutinizing, state with full conviction that he knows himself? There are two of us in every one of us, the conscious and the subconscious.

* * *

I believe that I believe I believe...

Bon Mots

Oxygen is modern man's oxen
With which he plows his very own existence

Hope is the soft pillow
Upon which the future rests

Tears are the overflow
of a reservoir of
genuine feeling

Justice is
Just – ice
Which melts away

It may be true that men are in the saddle.
However, it is the women who ride the horses.

To: Bed

You are more than a four-poster. You are the foundation of mankind. In miniature edition, you are offspring's crib, the cradle of civilization, the place where the human animal first lays eyes on this wondrous world. You furnish one of the few soft spots in our lives by providing a horizontal space where to cuddle, an area where we can escape from the reality of life. With you, we spend a third of our allotted time. Some of us are fortunate enough to fall easily asleep and dream. Others may lie awake and ponder. Basically, you are the place to gather strength for the next day.

You, we recall, as the spot where we were sent as a child, night after night. We thoroughly disliked you then because you took us away from listening to the talks of the grown-ups, which seemed to get so interesting just at that point. "Why can't I glance into the secret world of my parents?" we would say to ourselves. Why? But when sleep overtook us, these seemingly mysterious problems melted away. Dreams lead us into the splendor of Never-never Land.

With the years passing, we gradually learned to consider you to be the most private place in the house. With you, we did our thinking. A problem taken to you at night seemed to solve itself by morning. Somehow, you became Strategic Headquarters from which we directed our daily battle line-up. It was there where we felt the first stir of maturity.

As in life, many of your duties are unpleasant. Often you are transformed into a cave of pain. It is with you where humanity sweats out its measles, mumps and innumerable other diseases. You are the first witness to the birth of a child and you must listen to the outcries of agony. You hear prayers and curses. You cannot help but silently stand by when people become their own most aggressive enemy. It is with you where people lie awake for hours, worrying about yesterday and tomorrow while, had they given consideration to the present, it could have so much lightened their burden. It is with you where they die, provided that Providence did not catch up with them on the highway or the arm of death did not deprive you by pulling them away from behind the desk or other spot.

You never complain, however, no matter where you serve or whom you serve, be it to the rich or poor, prophet or prankster. You take it all in your stride. The most we can get out of you in the way of sentiment is a squeak at times.

Bed, somehow you have the qualities of a man in your massive, sturdy, protective appearance. You are so good to lean on. You, at your best, are Paradise; at your worst, you can well be compared to Inferno. All of us, your loyal patrons, have gotten a taste of both and thus a thorough indoctrination in life's every phase and a blurry gaze into what lies beyond.

Once you and your four posters are pulled away from us, we are dead!

From: A Bedfellow

Hands

What part of the human anatomy is more unique than our hands? Only human beings own hands. Animals have paws and claws, but certainly not hands.

Hands have fascinated great painters, sculptors and writers. Composers have set prose about them to musical notes. Who can ever forget those famous "Praying Hands" by Albrecht Dürer or the hands forming a cathedral by Auguste Rodin? Inspired by Rodin's "Cathedral," I wrote: I enter through the door near the thumbs into the majestic House of God, silenced only by the beatitude which speaks from its skyward frame. Ten magnificent pillars form its structure, providing all of life's thinking, feeling, which, when mixed together form life's oracle. God's sun is shining through the windows, these spaces in-between, where the pulsating life's blood seems to form the most beautiful stained-glass windows. Up on high is the cupola where the mysteries of the hands' secret skin design form paintings more beautiful than Michelangelo's. Down there in the soft palm I sit, hearing the organ music of my heartbeat, the choir of my soul which sings out so loud in voice and word. The Cathedral and I...we are bound together by God's band of silent language of baring his mysteries and yet, at the same time, veiling them.

Hands, those electrodes of the mind are able to relay the impulse of every human emotion. Often they appear not only to be in motion, but can seemingly be heard as well in applause. All of human thoughts find expression in them since they also act as constant interpreters.

It is in the palms of our hands where our destiny is written like an open book, waiting only to be deciphered by someone who understands that map.

The commandments, "Thou shalt not steal" and "Thou shalt not kill" are ultimately directed toward our hands, without which neither command could ever be broken.

Hands give, hands receive, hands welcome, hands say farewell, hands pray and hands curse, hands plead and hands thank, hands work and hands relax; they stroke and they strike; most of all, they write.

What would our hands be without the help of those valiant ten soldiers, our fingers? They are the ones who make them twinkle; they mimic, they point, they threaten, they question and they emphasize. Even when folded in death, hands express peace.

What is more miraculous than a baby's hand grasping the mother's finger? Or the hand of a father when it seems to speak loudly yes or no; could anything be more authoritive than that?

What language speaks the emotion-filled hand of a lover when it softly caresses its beloved? Where would the conductor be, the engineer, the doctor, the salesman; where would all of us be were it not for those God-given pair of hands?

Let us use them to applaud creation and re-creation, life itself. There is nothing handier than a pair of hands!

The Eyes Have It

Eyes undoubtedly are the most important exponent of our five senses. With them, we conceive the world around us; through them, we look out into the universe and at the same time into ourselves, our own inner world. Eyes are as talkative as our mouth, yet they never use the wrong word. Human eyes are no different from animal eyes when they plead, "Understand me, please."

Our eyes act as telegraphic messengers of our minds. They are constantly in motion, absorbing the life around them and teletyping their impressions to the brain. Often we look and yet we do not see. Many times, we see things not of immediate interest and pigeonhole these notions. Then too, no two pair of eyes see exactly the same thing, since each person absorbs impressions in his or her own way.

Just assume that blindness would befall mankind all over the entire world. All we know would be what we hear, smell, taste and feel. Being unable to see each other, hate would outlaw itself because, in the interest of survival, we could not afford it. Not being able to see, feeling would become one of our most important senses and our greatest asset, both types of feeling, the touch of our hands and the touch it makes upon our soul. We would not know about the existance of Mongols, Caucasians, Negroes, Melanesians and Polynesians. Human beings would be brother and sister to each other, no matter what their race or color. We cannot feel these differences through our hands and after a bath people smell alike. Whatever the shape of our eyes, it would not make a cock-eyed difference. Thus, we would have a much firmer basis from which to work towards world peace.

Oh, to what astounding use we could employ our eyes! Those precious mirrors of the soul can put reflections upon the mind which would cause humanity to move in the direction of global enlightenment. Terrible it is when seeing eyes leave no imprint upon a blind soul as when people remain unmoved by the suffering which they know is around them.

What is more sublime than eyes which say, I love you; you mean everything to me; you are mine until death do us part. Eyes which beg with just one tear in them. Eyes which wink at you and in a split second make you an ally.

Those two reflectors were given to us in order to see God's staging of his two-act drama: Life and Death.

The Siren and Sweet Whisperings

The other night when I walked through a park listening to the quiet murmur of the trees, a siren blew, reminding me of the naked life bordering this shelter of nature.

A siren speaks no language and yet its shrill voice tells an unmistakable story: disaster has struck. Maybe someone's house is on fire or some pedestrian was hit by a car. Good, I said to myself, the siren has finally stopped wailing; help must have come or is on the way. I thought what a strange phenomena it is that people are drawn toward such a scene rather than being thoroughly repulsed from such a debacle. I have heard of instances where the police were unable to aid a victim in time because curiosity seekers (oh yes, that is what they are) were blocking the avenue of approach.

I continued my walk through the park. Young couples, hand in hand, passed me in the semi-darkness and I could tell that my presence disturbed them as deeply as the siren had just affected me. They heard no murmur of the trees, as I did, because they were not alone. I had the trees and they had each other.

Parks are small strips of nature placed between cobblestones or streets. Sirens and sweet whisperings, I realized, are integral parts of my life.

The Ball

Every civilized person knows that the Earth is round. We can easily call it an Earth-ball. I wonder if the fascination the people of the world have with any round object does not stem from this psychological background.

Let's give this matter an eyeball of attention and recite those objects that keep us glued to the television screen, the stadiums, the golf courses, the tennis courts and what not, those attention getters which make women weekend widows.

Now I have to prove to you that I am on the ball, that I have a ball doing this scientific dissertation, that I am able to carry the ball and that I will play ball all along.

Let us therefore take the ballpoint pen in hand and get started: Tennis, anyone? Or perhaps Bowling, Base, Hand, Foot, Hard, Soft, High, Low, Billiard, Mazze, Spit, Inauguration, Cannon, Racquet, Golf, Glass, Pitch, Snow, Kick, Volley, Cricket, Surf, Butter, Tea, Bocce, Black or Ping Pong?

If you know of any other balls (Lucille Ball?), please let me know. In any case, I tried to hit the ball on the head. (Sorry Sir, I had to do it!)

Forgive me. It is enough to want to make you...bawl.

DAWN

And then morning came,
Rising from her slumber,
Birds greeting her with their call,
Humans were still down under.

How restful Nature is,
Yawning still from sleep,
A duck alone sounds human
And breaks the peace,
That day alone will turn to thunder.

What would life be without living,
Noise without its violent tone,
Love without giving,
Man without his throne?

There is design in this endless cycle,
The turning of dawn into dusk,
Mornings' glimmer becomes nights' glitter,
Nature, life...it is us.

Awake you Nature, sing you birds,
Man...hail the new day!
Just let me stand here, thinking,
Never, never go away.

Lake Tahoe

The sun just rose blushingly over the lake. This morning it has the surface of milk shortly before its boil. Quietness still engulfs this beautiful spot on earth; only seagulls seem to populate it – no boiling humanity yet. Nature too is a counterplay of contrasts. The early rising of the sun puts a rosy glimmer onto the blue-grey seriousness of the mountains, just as Man rises with renewed hope and delves into the tasks of a new day. At dusk, when the sun gradually sinks seemingly into nowhere with a mischievous blink as if to say nighty-night, you earthworms (behave if you can), see you in the morning.

Must there always be a nine-to-five chore with a seven-to-eleven reprieve and tiredness throughout? Must work and worry about the fate of Mankind becloud our minds?

To be pitied are they who have not learned to peel the fruit of life, bite into it, cherish its delicious juice and catapult its stone far into the distance.

There are the idealists who find it to be their life's work to change the pattern of the world by, what they term, peaceful means. Then there are the fighters who love to tangle and thus show their superiority. Do not let us forget the poor, mashed and mangled by life's burden, or the rich, who sacrifice living on the altar of their god, Moloch. Most important there are the artists to whom God gave an abundance of feeling, the sensitivity to hear their own blood pulsate.

Fortunate the person who knows not age or sickness and feels to be a living organism, to inhale and exhale the joy of Being.

Part VII
Novella

The Horizontal Point of View

For a long while I had been thinking how nice it would be to have a few months of time all to myself without the worry of making a living and without having to keep up with the requirements of society (including cocktail parties, no matter how wet, yet so dry). Little did I know that this opportunity would present itself in an entirely different form than ever imagined.

When Moses went up Mt. Sinai, God gave him the Ten Commandments. When I went up Mt. Hood in Oregon, He gave me ten weeks in traction.

My family and I were returning from a ski trip on New Years Day when the accident happened. This was not my idea of how the New Year should start.

I was standing only two feet away from the spot where one of the most friendly and helpful young men one can encounter was killed while in the process of showing his good neighborliness. I feel that I can extend to him, this finest of all friends, no greater a tribute than to pay homage right here, although our friendship on earth lasted only two minutes. While bending down to remove tire chains from our family car which I had parked behind his, this young man was mortally hit while I broke my upper thigh from the result of being squeezed in between the two cars.

Even though we were legally parked on the right soft shoulder of the highway with a clean, clear highway on both sides, the lethal driver with her mind somewhere else veered right into us. Seeing the car coming, I thought it could not be, but before I had time for a second reaction I felt myself falling and screamed, "My leg! My leg!" I was planning to take a business trip three weeks hence and oddly, it somehow flashed through my mind that this was out of the question.

The next thing I knew, my fifteen-year-old daughter, Fay, was whimpering over me and I tried to comfort her. People descended from all around. A registered nurse was bending over me and claimed to know me although I could not recall her.

149

There was a patch on her shirt sleeve that said she was a member of an Olympic team. A medical doctor inquired if I would want a shot of morphine and I felt that could do me no harm. First-aiders covered me with blankets but they did not realize that I was lying on the bare street.

Only then did I see my wife standing there, her face covered with blood, but she assured me that she was not seriously hurt. Looking to the left down the street, I saw the body of our friend, whose friendship lasted not longer than a flash of lightning, yet whose human quality impressed itself deep enough to be with me always as a symbol of the goodness of man. His example will be a shining light forever.

This was certainly not the way I had pictured the circumstances of my retreat. It would have been closer to my expectations had I wrenched my neck while looking after a stunning blonde walking in the opposite direction, but life is not that simple. Wishes don't always come true exactly as planned. I wanted to write and give vent to some inner voice. What I would write or how good it might be was of no concern. Thus, my confinement was chosen for me.

On my bedside lay Harry Golden's book, *Enjoy, Enjoy.* I liked his style. When his first book, *Only In America,* came out, I felt that here was another man who felt and wrote as I did. That is what America needs, I thought, a down-to-earth, sentimental writer who presents the many problems of human life in a simple, cheerful way; who writes about life, not fiction, about real people, not men from Mars. Forgive me when I add my own "one cent's worth."

I so well remember when still in school how we would make tests in physics class on the attraction of the magnetic field. We would put hundreds of little iron pieces on a flat surface, then hold a magnet close to them and the most amazing turnabout would occur. Only yesterday I was a simple man, an average American as they say, going about my business and my pleasures in a fairly unobtrusive way. Although I had gone through difficult times – losing my mother and brother in Auschwitz and Sobibor infamous concentration camps – fate smiled at me in the form of success, health and a happy family. In my profession, I had the opportunity to dispense leadership coupled with kindness. In addition, I had the privilege to be part and parcel of a growing organization doing what I was trained to do. "Cast the bread upon the water and it will return manifold"...which brings me back to the magnetic field.

Yesterday, I was one of those hundreds of iron kernels floating about. Today, I made the headlines, not as a Nobel Prize winner (which would have been more to my liking), but as a victim and survivor of an accident on the highway. Suddenly the attention of hundreds of people, most of whom I had met only casually, turned in my direction just as the magnetized iron kernels. People reached for the telephone or sat down to write a note, sent flowers or candy. Suddenly, for one day, I had become the center of attention, the pinnacle. A human side of the magnitude of the Fata Morgana on the heavens was displayed. The well-veiled and hidden human heart suddenly showed crystal clear through the vestments. Barriers of competition, social strata, religious and racial background were no more. Prayers brought out a unity, a strength, a wave upon which I recovered.

Why is it that only a tragedy can evoke human feelings? What can be done in an emergency on the highway could and should equally be done in relation to people as a whole.

The colorful and the colorless, as Harry Golden classifies Americans so significantly, can learn to get along together, if properly taught. All people are basically decent. People are the same everywhere who want a roof above their heads and a meal upon the table for themselves and for their children. While we worry if AT&T will split again one for three, most people would be happy to have the bare essentials. Why should the Russian people or the Chinese or any other people be different in their goals? The people in Russia are no more atheistic than others. Even the most primitive people anywhere believe in something superior to themselves, no matter what name is given to it.

What good are atomic bombs or missiles other than giving their producers a feeling of protection without which large nations apparently cannot be? "A big stick" was the most effective weapon in Theodore Roosevelt's time and continues to be so until this day. What a blessing it would be if once again, instead of spending money on nuclear reactors, we could devote more time and money to exploring uncharted territories in the scientific field. The greatest enemy of all people is poverty. Weapons do not destroy poverty but enhance it. Once we realize that it is machinery and technical know-how which can change third-world countries, bloodless battles will be won, there will be an improvement of living conditions for all and a genuine feeling of friendship will develop between countries.

Standing on the top of a magnificent hill only an hour before being tossed into the abyss, I reflected on the glory of this bountiful world, the azure sky above scattered with playful white clouds and the snow-covered mountains sticking up like sugarheads all around. I pondered for a moment on how fortunate my family and I had been during the past quarter century, how little we actually let the many disturbing factors touch us. We were healthy, beseeched of few illnesses, with our children alert and sound in mind. My mood of reflection was equal if not superior to a prayer uttered out loud: God, you have blessed me with ever-full hands; it simply cannot be that I will endlessly be spared of further hardships. I wondered when my day of reckoning would come. Since God seemingly for unknown reasons punishes only the good and the best and since I prided myself to have a bit of the devil within me, I felt protected. Did I have qualities which I believed were not there? I got hit. I am sharing the burden of the blessed ones.

Only a few weeks prior to these happenings, I started to prepare my own eulogy. "No man shall write my epitaph." Approaching the half-century mark of age, I felt that it was time to pause for it. Somehow, this is a family tradition. My grandfather on my mother's side wrote his own last words, even though I have never seen them or heard about the contents. I was only four years old when he passed away, yet I always had the thought in mind that I owed such a gesture to myself. Why add to the burden of the religious leader on that fateful day with the chore of saying nice things about someone who, as often as not, he had hardly known? If there were achievements to be booked on the credit-side of the human ledger during his lifetime, they should have been shouted from the rooftops long ago. Why waste a whole new page when it has become meaningless? Eulogies, I believe, should not have as a subject matter the deceased. It is he who should leave behind a message, an ideal for others to continue to follow. It is he who should tell them how futile their lives have been if never once invaded by a heavenly spark. What are all material things accumulated and left behind compared to one line like Keats', "A thing of beauty is a joy forever." That sentence and many other literary contributions add more to the aesthetic way of life than all the gold in Fort Knox.

Yes, the girl who hit me came to visit in the hospital. I did not know her name then, nor did I ask it. I had forgiven her and asked God's blessings upon her. She incapacitated me for awhile and, even though she came out of it without a scratch, her soul must be affected for life by the involuntary manslaughter of a fine and innocent young man. I appreciated the fact that she had the decency and the courage to face me. Oh, how so many would have hidden behind the mask of their lawyer, eliminating all human emotions in favor of immunity.

It does the heart good to see that there is some warmth left in this sometimes seemingly cold world.

* * *

Finding myself tied down to a hospital bed seemed very much like a sudden decision to join an order of monks. Goodby outside world, place of murder on the highway, killings and robberies which constitute the daily headlines of the newspaper. Suddenly all is sublime. Angels in white uniforms flit about distributing bedside pills along with an atmosphere of peace and friendliness. The doctors "play God" by their direct and final decisions of what to do, when and how. Everything is activity from the orderlies on up to the Head Nurse. The passives are the patients. They are the victims, pounced upon with needles, thermometers, syringes and wonderfully bloody operations. Tape and bandages! Oh, how the nurses love to see you cringe when they remove them ever so slowly. Last but not least, let me tell you about those bedpans. I had heard of fur-lined bathtubs and could not see much use in them. Now, if they had invented fur-lined bedpans, they certainly would have done me a particular favor!

Impossible to pass up the nurses with only one or two words. The old saying that a man would get off his deathbed to chase a nurse takes on stark reality here. This is simply a matter of observation and does not include the writer because... because he could not get off the bed. It was my neighbor in the next bed who made the keen observation that apparently only the best looking girls take up the nursing profession. Without having long-enough experience to judge properly, I can, however, state frankly that nurses are sort of a lifeline between a drowning sailor and his ship; they dispense smiles; they are femininity, a nutrient every man needs at breakfast, lunch, dinner, morning, noon and night. Just like oxygen, women become an integral part of our breathing. Not being a woman, I cannot say for sure if this same feeling holds true in relation of women towards men. Somehow, I have the feeling that this is not quite so. Women are the ones who give life. They are the source, the spring from which life is brought forth. We, the males, are the eternally ejected ones, separated forever. Somehow, in our behavior with the opposite sex, we seem to want to return from whence we came. We seem to want to re-establish contact. We grope just like a baby. We, the strong sex (what a farce!), need support, recognition and love. This is, I believe, that which we seem to chase all of our lives.

* * *

Antoinette Hatfield, wife of the Governor of Oregon, sent me a get-well note today. I like to call her, "the Governess" and I hope she will not hold it against me. This is one of the sweetest girls you can meet and her story is the "Cinderella story" itself. In Mark Hatfield, she found her prince and together they made sure that he was elected governor. He is a fine, handsome man, the kind you expect to come across in fiction land. The amazing thing is that his outside qualities are well-matched, if not surpassed, by his great abilities.

It was he who gave one of the introductory speeches to the election of Richard Nixon at the Republican Convention; that committee realized that nowhere could they find a better speaker and personality. I have heard Mark speak several times on various occasions and was enthralled each time by his precise presentation and warm personality which flow from the rostrum like a mist of Chanel No. 5. As I said before, there is no successful man without a woman behind him to push him on. Mark could not be quite the man he is without Antoinette. Their story, I have always felt, is a special one. Somehow, it had to be they.

* * *

Time to reflect on the wonderful people with whom I am sharing (when on two healthy legs) the daily experience and yes, the privilege of working. There are many people with whom the only direct contact is a "good morning" or a "good night." In the business of business, there is often no private word exchanged, even with the people one consults daily. A smile, a little jibe while passing by in the zig-zag of daily activity (which seems to follow a pattern of shooting stars, seemingly without direction) makes all the difference. The customer, though not on the payroll, is the real honest-to-goodness boss. The customer determines the atmosphere of the day. If there is a frown on his or her brow, the sales clerk feels it and the manager is brought out to unwrinkle that crease. The most tragic situation is when a customer comes in and says, "I could have died last night when I received your package and found a teaspoon in place of a salad fork!" Imagine. While the State Department is desperately trying to avert war in Cuba, this customer could have died because she received the wrong piece of silver. Oh, these are such serious matters, hard to describe and yet to the individual, the matter of The Salad Fork is of much greater importance than Cuba far away.

I have often wondered by which law it happens that when we open the door in the morning, customers step over the threshold. Magazines often state that they have a readership of two million people. What were to happen were a goodly number of them suddenly in the mood to storm the store at the same time? As long as the customers come – and the more the merrier – we are happy. We need these darlings, no matter in what frame of mind they come to see us. We are the doctor, they are the patients (some may need a little more attention than others). Our advice, our friendliness, our service, our expert knowlege go a long way. The customer with the frown needs more attention, not less. Oh, how grateful they become once they are shown understanding. Many women have a domineering husband and have absolutely nothing to say at home. Now, while shopping, they are on their own; they are on the loose, their only chance to rule someone else. Let them, I tell my co-workers; don't fight them; it makes them happy. It is a very inexpensive way to bring some happiness into their lives and a profitable one for us since we create lifelong customers and often close personal friends.

No, I have not forgotten you, my co-workers, you people who share the great part of my working life. I spend more time with you than I do with my wife and my children. You make my world. The way we react together forms the basis of not only my life, but also of yours. The greatest feeling with which a person can be instilled is looking forward to getting up in the morning. (Some of you do household chores at 5:00 AM, I am told). The eagerness to get on the job, to do the day's work willingly and with pleasure, to always be able to put yourself in that frame of mind is one of the greatest of blessings. It is that eagerness which makes it difficult to lie here. Fortunately, I have found less important occupations I am able to perform, such as putting these thoughts on paper and learning Italian via pictures. Keeping busy is the most excellent therapy. Whatever anybody does, from the charwoman on up, you must always feel that you are the captain of your ship, that it is up to you to sail it well. Life's successes and failures, happiness and unhappiness, lie in our own two little hands. Only by realizing this can we steer the ship well over the buoyant tossing of our individual oceans. Let us learn to take responsibility for our actions. Let us be free men and women always. Oh yes, I do know how often we are inclined to say, "What is the use of it all? Who cares if I work harder or if I give more of myself?" That is exactly where the secret of living is buried. By giving more, you enrich yourself. Even if at times you seemingly cannot satisfy your superior, you can always satisfy yourself which is the most important factor in life. If on the way, you can stir the satisfaction of others, so much the better.

Granted, I am laid up with my leg high in the air, isolated from the outside world and dependent on the goodness and kindness of the hospital staff. Yet, I maintain the liberty of letting my mind travel thousands of miles away if I so desire, or just a few blocks. As long as the mind is alive and awake, there is no cause for pity.

"The Horizontal Point of View." That is the title I have selected for my discourse. Things look entirely different from this position, I dare say more level-headed. Pride, one of the phenomena of the vertical position, finds no comfort here.

Rather humility becomes one's bed companion, the stroke of luck to be alive, to be partaker in the fruits of life, to be able to see light, hear noises, feel the touch of a hand, to taste good food and smell spring in the air via beautiful flowers. How the stocks on comfort suddenly rise to soaring heights. Yesterday I was part of it all. Today, I am parted, separated.

For the first time in ever so long, I watched a most amazing spectacle: when dusk turns into night, signaling the end of another day and when dawn turns into morning, proclaiming a new day full of hope and expectations. Yes, it is that hope under any circumstances which keeps us pushing forward, even if it consists only of the ability of pushing a pencil forward on a piece of white paper. What could be better therapy than watching a beautiful sunrise and what could restore a more peaceful elation than the gradually disappearing pink colorplay on the horizon?

One can meet the most interesting people quartered in a hospital ward. A new man showed up in the bed beside me. He is a very kind man, simple and yet with a most interesting life history. He comes of pioneer stock somewhere in the mountains of Idaho from a piece of land, a homestead, that his father, his grandfather and their fathers before them inhabited and cultivated. He said so wisely, "I should never have left my father's home. I would be so much better off today."

He did leave, however, many years ago to become an electrician and was nearly electrocuted on the job. He still suffers from the aftereffects today. We city slickers do not realize that there are many of these successors of pioneers toiling on their farms who are happy doing just that. He told me of the times when the check in payment for the raw wool shorn from the sheep represented new clothing for the kids. Although the workday on the farm was fourteen to fifteen hours long, there was always enough food to eat. One of the brothers would hire himself out sixty hours a week for twelve dollars to bring in a bit of cash whenever its scarcity made itself felt during the "good old days." (Many of us can remember in all probability a twelve-dollar compensation during the thirties – the good old days – in the cities as well.) They bought a Model-T Ford, vintage 1926, for the price of sixteen dollars, one dollar down and the balance over fifteen months, and they had a rough time meeting those payment dates. That car, however, meant contact with the outside world; it took them to fishing holes and hunting grounds; it also brought home the meat from deer and elk-hunting excursions.

Even a simple man's life cannot remain simple. When the crane on which my roommate was working accidentally hit a high tension wire, electricity burned him nearly to the point of death. He was taken to the hospital and confined there for a year while the doctors grafted and re-grafted his skin. Feeling lonely, he fell in love and married the young nurse who took care of him, believing that her feelings were genuine. What was actually in her mind, he found out later to his great dismay, is that she imagined a fifty-thousand-dollar settlement with the state for his accident. Since her little hand had never held a dollar bill exceeding two figures, she thought that this would set her up for the rest of her life. As it turned out, the state was not too eager to dispense with that kind of money. Her attempts in cahoots with some tavern owner to declare her husband legally insane luckily failed since the District Attorney did not comply. All this happened while this man was flat on his back. Once he was released, he found that most of his possessions were gone before his so-called wife could flee the state. He began divorce proceedings.

Why do I talk about this incident? Every individual life is an interesting one.

There was another new man in the bed next to me in the process of repairing frostbite on one of his injured feet. No one ever came to see him; he was not flooded with flowers and phone calls, as I was, because there was hardly anyone who cared enough. Then too his family – mother, father and brethren – lived out of town. I begged him to take some of my many flower pots for his bedside. We shared magazines, a luxury to which he was not accustomed. I knew how much he loved nature, flowers, animals, the woods and streams. Fortunately, these were compensation for him. He loved to paint in oil and he told me about the many pictures he had done of mountains, deer and horses. He expressed himself this way and eased his burden. Not many people are able to pursue a hobby to release their tensions. Take a hint from someone who has been lying in the middle of a hospital bed for many months: find a relaxation away from your daily business procedures; ride a horse, collect stamps, work with wood or leather, whatever it is, just so it is something to maintain your mental and physical equilibrium.

*　*　*

Somehow I feel that I should compensate you, the reader, for the valuable time you are spending in interpreting these lines. Here is a remedy on how to keep insects away from your home: plant two insect-eating tulips at opposite ends of your garden. Their fragrance will attract all insects and keep your home free of them. If you have trouble with moles unearthing your grass, I have learned that there is a certain plant which, by its smell, drives the pesty animals in opposite directions, right into your neighbor's yard.

If any of you, my friends, believe that I was bored, I must disappoint you. I absolutely was not. Get yourself in a little traffic jam and join me, won't you?

One day a young nurse came into my room, looked at the stretching gear on my left leg and said with the driest of faces, "It looks that you are in for a stretch." I liked that pun since I not only like to listen to them, but manufacture them occasionally. When I invent one at home, my family holds their noseholes closed and yet when Bob Hope (forgive me, Bob, your reputation is established) uses the same pun, everybody enjoys it thoroughly. That goes to show you.

Speaking of holes, looking up to the ceiling I see sound tiles with twenty holes one way and twenty the other. I could easily figure out how many holes there are on the entire ceiling, but I am here to recuperate and to stretch my leg, not my brain. I only now realize how important openings are to us. Without the draw-curtain effect of our eyelids, we would not be able to see; without the ear-holes, we would not hear; without the pores in our skin, we would not be able to breathe and feel; nor are the nose and mouth openings to be thought away. What good is a wall without an opening for a door? Where would daylight be in the house were it not for the window? This was not always an established fact. Some of you might remember the story of the burghers who built a house without windows and then tried to bring in the daylight with buckets. If someone were to erect a monument to nothingness, it might as well be I.

* * *

Looking out through the glass-covered window of my room, which has become my outside world for many a day now, I enjoy the abundance of beauty which represents itself in that small strip. The coloration on a sunny day (though there have been very few) is beyond description. I see mountains, the sky, moving cars on a highway which represents the city life. Yes, though confined, it is a great blessing to know that I am still part of it all and that someday in the near future once again I will be able to roam the ground freely.

It would be as easy for me to picture the other side of my life. I could tell of agonies encountered, of blood and pains. There is absolutely no market for that kind of commodity and then too I know that only by a positive way of thinking can I aid the healing process. The doctor told me of two identical cases he had treated where one patient survived and the other passed on for this reason only.

Often it is said, "Is it not a terrible world we live in?" This is so absolutely wrong since the world itself has changed very little and whatever changes have taken place give no interference to us. The world is the same beautiful world; it is us, the people who trod on it who come and go, who have not found the denominator yet to peaceful living. It is we the people who create an atmosphere of strife, not the world.

Lying here with a white bedsheet slung about me and a watch upon my arm, I inherited at least the physical implements of one of the greatest human beings of our time, Mahatma Ghandi. These were his only earthly possessions, yet he was the richest man alive. Mahatma means "Little White Father," the only honor which he ever wanted bestowed upon him. He was the Little White Father to millions of people in India who, under the overlordship of the English, were kept in poverty. How can a weak people overthrow a colossus, well-fed and armed to the teeth? Only a great mind and a humanitarian alike could figure out ways and means in a slow but steady process to overthrow the iron master. Ghandi preached passive resistance, an entirely new concept of warfare. By his example, he carried his people with him. In a way, he ridiculed the English in their self-satisfaction, by showing that his ideals were far superior and worthy of emulation. Long before I became imbedded with "the horizontal point of view," I was deeply impressed with his philosophies as mind over matter is the problem that the Western world faces so seriously every day.

To develop one's own mind, we have to learn to be alone with ourselves and that is a challenge. Indeed, to be able to concentrate means to be able to be alone with oneself. Every person should devote from five to ten minutes every single day in the state of complete relaxation simply by sitting down to reflect. If at first you have no thoughts, stare holes into the air. You will always remember these moments as having breathed consciously, of having lived. So many people die after an active life without ever really having taken time out to live.

* * *

My inner ear hears the voice of my wife saying, "Paul, take a month of vacation. I think that you need a rest." I look at her and say to myself what a strange thing to think up. Take a month's vacation? She must be plumb out of her head. How can I, a busy man, entertain such thoughts? I have work to do which requires my presence always.

So what happens? The next day I get hit by a car and the verdict is three months in the hospital. Three months! What can I do about it? Fate is fate. Take a month's vacation? Don't be silly; it simply cannot be done!

Such is the relativity of life. *Che sarà sarà.* Were we to actually realize this hair-thin thread on which all of us dangle, how could anybody act snobbish or impertinent at any time during his life? When a coin drops, it shows one of its two sides. This, however, does not eliminate the other side. How could I ever have had the faintest idea of the real, true compassion which grips people or know of their genuine devotion and interest had I not put them to a test. Phone calls and letters tell me that the outside line did not stand still for days at the place where I worked. Greatness is within us if we only uncork it and let it freely flow.

I met so many fine women who devote one day a week to helping in the hospital, dispensing books or coffee, who will do anything that might be required at a particular time. These people cherish their own health and pay tribute simply by contributing.

What might be a mishap to one brings luck to others. Today we were joined by a third man. He works in the Trust Department of a local bank. What could be more interesting than to delve into deeds and oversee loot that is still buried in the vaults, valuables which might date from the first horsethief who came to Oregon long, long ago. The AT&T shares which Grandpa bought are still lying there with nobody daring to sell them since they might still go up and one would rather let them rot then pay Uncle Sam his share. There is the jewelry of every dame who ever lived in this state, buried, buried. Who wants the stuff anyway, it is so outmoded? Then there are the deeds, the good, the bad and the real-estate deeds which make sure that Johnny, the grandson of that yet unborn daughter, will be well fixed.

Lying here I realize what a boon I must be to the economy. I wonder if Babson has included me in his forecast? What would the hospital industry have done without my case? They would have to peddle the bed for a hatching place of chickens. Who would keep paying the laundry bill for the immaculate white uniforms of the nurses, the orderly, the water dispenser, the blood taker? There are the doctors, wonderfully devoted men, who dispense not only their knowledge and their encouragement but, in addition, every minute of their working lives. There is hardly an industry that is not affected by my dismay: the lawyers, the insurance agents and maybe even the tavern on the corner where (who knows?) my friends might be assembled drinking down their grief about my predicament.

The fireworks are still to come. In a few months, the legal battle will flare. Just as two men used to defend their honor by meeting at dawn in some field outside the community to perform a shooting match, so will the lawyers meet in the courtroom to shoot words at each other until one of them is out-maneuvered, out-argued and pierced into pieces by the arrows of logic and reasoning.

Thinking about all of this, I realize how nice the simple matter of taking a walk again, even on crutches, would be, maybe to a nearby park. To walk under those majestic trees on little paths sidled with fern, one of the oldest of plants, and to hear the song of the birds, which must be messages of love, would be heavenly. All is so peaceful there. Or is it? The bird catching a worm, a living thing, to still its hunger. Is this such a peaceful-appearing nature when every living thing is in search of food or in flight from some danger? No animal is really fully protected; no life insurance there; all is eat or be eaten. Yet, all looks so peaceful. I guess we have learned not to see the continuous war that is going on around us. If it teaches us anything, it is that life is just a cycle, like cycle-billing with a balance owed. Injuries like mine should serve as a warning signal such as we find at a railroad crossing: Stop – Look – Listen.

Life is very much like a stageplay. It is the action between the lifting and falling of the curtain. When we watch a play, we identify with the actors; they play our life for us; they fulfill the dreams which are within us; they express the hope which we carry in our hearts. Attending a fight or a race, we take in the display of strength we would like to possess. Then we act out our own play; we add laughter to the comedy and sentimental words to the tragedy. All the while, we are only vaguely aware that ours is just a short performance.

* * *

Is there a market for writings? I should have asked myself that question before starting out with this treatise, hopefully a tease-treat. Judging by the enormous book sales which are periodically announced in the newspapers, this at one-half of one-half of the original price, brain power is priced very low. Add to this the thousands of manuscripts which never find their way to the publisher, one must come to the conclusion that writing in most cases is a dilemma. But then, doing what one wants to do is the best therapy. How many leather-tooled objects and woven mats are lying around in attics which were produced under similar circumstances? The step between the marketplace and the garbage truck is only a small one.

* * *

Today is my birthday. Imagine, celebrating a birthday in a

hospital bed, of all places. My family and closest friends are gathered around the foot of the bed. A birthday cake is on the bed tray with just enough candles to match my blowing-out power. Everybody is singing the traditional "Happy Birthday." As we lift the imaginary glass of champagne, everyone toasts my health, of which I will need lots of in the days to come. I imagine a ring of Baccarat glasses forming waves to encircle all of my friends not present both near and far.

* * *

Pain is the ingredient of sickness. No matter how many pills they give you, there will be nights when you cannot sleep. Naturally we would not really know what pain is had we not experienced at one time or another the sense of joy. Oh, what a comfort, what a deep relief it is when in moments of pain, your mind can call back instances of utter delight. I have come to the conclusion that we are granted joy for the express purpose of forming a buffer, a soft mental pillow, upon which to rest easier. Honest and truly, what would life amount to were it not for the few trophies which adorn our mental shelf?

I have just been informed that an operation is necessary to bring the two broken bones properly together. Even though this is not a serious matter, an operation is what the word implies. Only by a strong effort to keep your head high (not quite so difficult when the headpiece of the bed is rolled up), can one counteract the many cross-currents which flow through the mind by the mere mentioning of that word. As is demanded of us so often in life, once again we must conquer ourselves. If ever a man looked forward to such an ordeal, it was I. The weights which proved not to have done the job properly became unbearable and I preferred the surgical incision to what seemingly had become the weight of the Brooklyn Bridge.

Punctually at 10:00 AM, the nurse gave me the first injection to put me to sleep. Fortunately, it was decided to move me to the operating room in my bed, Brooklyn Bridge and all. There I met the anesthetist, Mr. Green. Mr. Green meet Mr. Lavender. What a colorful world this is! They propped me on one side to bare my back. Then they marked the various points of my spine which required an injection to numb the lower part of my body. As soon as this was done, all feeling disappeared and I was ready. They strapped me onto the table and inserted the needle for the dextrose and blood plasma where I could observe its steady flow. At times during the four hour and ten minute siege, I was awake. I felt the vibration of the hammering and chiselling on my bones although I fortunately had no other feelings. When I woke up once again, I found myself in the recovery room sans the Brooklyn Bridge. I felt extremely thirsty but was allowed to chew only on a rag. There was too much danger of you-know-what. Gradually, my good right leg woke up and I winked at the nurses by wiggling my toes at them. My left foot, which was laying in a cradle like a newborn baby, took a bit longer to extricate from slumber. I asked if I could move my arms, which they graciously permitted, and it was a pleasure indeed to attend to that itch on the top of my nose. Soon the free parking here was over and I was wheeled back into my room. On the way, I heard the tones of a radio somewhere which gave me the good feeling that I was not in heaven where, I hope, they have not yet switched to rock 'n roll.

There she was, my wife, a most welcome sight. I just moved my hand from under the cover to indicate that I would like hers nestled in mine. At such a moment, the current which flows between us, two people in love, is life giving.

Soon I was permitted to have the small doses of water that I craved and what balsam they were. Just as a mother bird puts a worm into the mouth of her young fledgling, so my wife dispensed the liquid worm to me.

Gradually life and pain were returning. I tried to divert my thoughts from the pain by intensive reading, writing, listening to the radio and looking at television, all welcome time-shorteners. I made a most interesting observation. During the first few weeks, I had the innate desire to be creative, to write rather than listen. As my condition gradually improved, this desire for activity slowly changed into passivity. The radio and television I had successfully banned from my room for several weeks, now became desirable bedside companions with the "good music" station during the day and a good television channel at night. I still cannot rid myself of the feeling that television is crippling whole nations with its gluing effect. In all these years, I have come to really enjoy only one program, the appearance of Bishop Sheen (and that must be the reason they took it off the air.) I consider him one of the finest human beings of our time, a religious man, yet free enough to extoll a sense of humor embracing all humanity.

My entire welfare depends on the correct balancing of my leg in the cradle, held by a hoist. Just as a logger determines the precise balance of a piece of timber by setting the boom correctly, so the hoist had to be set right to assure my comfort. With the doctors giving the instructions and the orderlies executing them in their own fashion, I found the interpretations with my leg left hanging painfully in the middle. My friend from the country was a logger among many other professions and was instrumental in finally properly conveying the correct angle of the hoist to the attendant, thus greatly lessening my discomfort. Soon my bed neighbor will be released and I can only wish that he will find a world friendly and helpful toward his ventures.

It took three weeks from the day of my confinement until I felt that I was gradually coming out of the stupor which had enslaved me. The injections and many pills created a kind of haze that left me feeling as if I were in a vacuum. Someone brought me an issue of *Playboy*, that naughty magazine, and, by golly, it seemed to rouse interest. This is, I believe, a better measure of a person's health than the doctor's stethoscope. Coming out can well be compared to the famous fairytale in which the princess awakens after a hundred-year sleep and this through the kiss of her prince. Yes, I too was kissed, kissed by the return of life, the rising of the sun which suddenly took on new beauty and the smiles of the nurses. Dormant, pleasant memories started to awaken and linked together the illustrious past with the present, creating new hopes for the future. The assignment for me is complete recovery. Like an ambassador preparing for his post, I am getting ready to fulfill my duty to myself by recovering completely.

* * *

Today is Inauguration Day. John Fitzgerald Kennedy is being inaugurated, the youngest and seemingly the most vigorous president ever elected. This is the seventh time a president had been inaugurated since my coming to the United States, yet it is the first time that I have found the opportunity to attend the ceremony via television. It was an accident which afforded me the rare opportunity to watch a proceeding which most Americans have to forego. Apparently nothing is so bad that it does not carry a kernel of good within itself. I hereby propose that we sacrifice a minor holiday every four years in favor of a legal Inauguration Day and make it a national holiday. Even though only a small majority of the people went to the polls, the president becomes the president of all Americans.

It was interesting to see notables from every country in the world assembled and the private fashion show their wives put on. Have you ever contemplated what an enormous undertaking it is to put such a spectacle on the road? Every single participant's ego has to be carefully wrapped in cotton so that it does not get hurt during the process. Rank has to be carefully preserved.

It gave me a wonderful feeling to hear Marion Anderson sing the National Anthem. I can remember the days when it took Mrs. Eleonore Roosevelt, the greatest of emancipated women, to speak out loudly against the bigots who tried to refuse such an artist this privilege. We have come a long way and it feels good to see progress and to gradually find other such artists accepted. Still, we have to remind ourselves that it took courageous, really free people to bring us here.

The appearance of Robert Frost, a fine old man whose eyes gave out just at the crucial moment, aroused two thoughts within me: the dark mantle which gradually falls around the shoulders of all of us and, looking at the young leader, the stark contrast between the two men, poet and politician.

Why was President Kennedy's speech hailed as such a good one all over the globe? It was simplicity itself, basic to the problems of people all over the world. We will help, he said, provided you will lend a hand in helping yourselves. I am dedicated to the betterment of all people, friend or foe, because only by elimination of poverty can we protect the rights of the rich at the same time. By ejecting idolatry, bigotry and hatred, only by conquering these can we reach our ultimate goal, peace everywhere.

Right now President and Mrs. Kennedy are riding up Constitution Avenue to their new home, the White House. The people, in a happy, festive mood, are cheering loudly. President Kennedy must think, "It would be nice were these people the Senate and the Congress to remain cheering, even when the tax collector comes along."

It is only a tiny step from reality to fiction. A few days later, I saw a charming program on television which dealt with potentates from fiction land. Richard Boone, in the program "Have Gun Will Travel," was hired by the prince of a small country to find the young princess who had just been kidnapped while visiting San Francisco. It was assumed that she was on her way to Mexico. Mr. Boone got busy, jumped on his horse and pretty soon discovered a campsite where two men and a young girl were moving around. With Boone's ingenuity, it did not take him long to get the two fellows to jump onto their horses and flee into the wild blue yonder. This left him alone with the princess, who was expressing royalty with every inch of her. Boone told her that he was hired to take her back to San Francisco, which displeased her. When night fell, they each slept in their separate tents and endured the howling of the wolves. Fear brought the princess closer to where Boone was bedded. Awakening in the morning, she felt his arm around her in a protective way, which she, however, resented. It was moving to see how she gradually gained trust and confidence towards this older, tough but gentle man. She told him of the strict ways in which she was brought up, of how years were spent in teaching her how to sit properly, walk royally, everything...and that emotions were taboo. She confided that even she, a princess, had feelings and that she had fallen in love with him. Boone, master of every imaginable temptation, seemingly could not conquer this one. They fell into each other's arms rather vehemently with Boone quoting an array of classical wisdoms, including one stating that "duty is the shadow of man."

Both had a duty to perform, a duty which neither of them could escape. Together they returned to San Francisco, where the princess resumed her royal duties and Boone prepared to go to his next assignment. While her subjects knelt before her, the princess met Boone's eyes for the last time and with a wink, they parted; a wink, I believe, which will sustain both of them for the rest of their lives because they were graced to experience the deepest of human emotions and master it.

A few days later, I watched Leonard Bernstein explaining romance in music. In composing too, we yearn for freedom, disciplined freedom, he said, which is the basic implement of democracy.

The word, discipline, which up to this time I felt had escaped the American language and the American way of life, suddenly appeared strongly in all three instances – John F. Kennedy's address, the little fictional story and the words of Leonard Bernstein. I believe we have started a new era in our way of thinking and that new feelings of disciplined freedom will be our final salvation.

Must not forget my leg though. It is right in front of me in the cradle and the doctor says that it is getting along very nicely. Thank you, Doctor...and God.

* * *

Today I had two important visitors, one cancelling out the other; the Orthodox Rabbi and the resident Chaplain of the Episcopalian faith. Spiritual guidance is important, especially when you are in a position where the mind is being negatively taxed with racing pain. These men did not dispense religion though, which you might think that they would do. They just wanted me to know that I was being watched over. In the final analysis, they report to the same Superior and their oppositeness down here really does not make an iota of difference up there. I believe that each religion travels a different road with their spiritual leader at the head, but that all roads lead to the same end-station, just as in London, every road seems to lead to Piccadilly Circus and in Paris to the Tomb of the Unknown Soldier.

Looking out the window, I see two magnificent components, the heavens and the earth. They are tremendous bodies which seem to move independently from each other; just as the human being in his thoughts establishes contact between himself and the heavens, so does, no doubt, a relationship exist between Mother Earth and Father Heaven. When rain falls, it is welcome nectar to the earth, the plant and the flower. Flashes of lightning which dance like a polka on the sky during a hot summer night can be compared to the majestic beauty of a dozen roses given by a lover to a beloved. These are but the overture, the gentle flirting, which gradually turns into forceful insistence when the growling of rolling thunder can be heard beyond the mountains. Lightning strikes and finds release in the drenching of the earth by the rain. Thunder again rolls off as an aftermath, Nature's applause to herself for a job well done, as once more storm turns into rain, as sweet as only a farewell kiss can be.

* * *

An actor friend of mine sent a picture of himself in the role of Franklin Delano Roosevelt, whom he portrayed in "Sunrise at Campobello." He played that role so superbly that any similarity between FDR and the actor seems no longer accidental. The photograph, now framed, is standing on the dresser in front of me, serving as a constant reminder that there was a man who suffered more greatly than I, yet was able to handle the wheel of time so well.

Coming back to the situation at hand, nothing is longer than a sleepless night. It is not quite so amusing as it sounds when the nurse enters the room and wakes you up in order to give you a sleeping pill. In desperation, you might turn on an all-night radio station and towards morning, listen to yesterday's hog-price quotations.

As the healing progresses, feelings of loneliness make their appearance. I miss the home, the loving family, the daily contact with the public, the people who are my neighbors, nodding acquaintances on the bus, the customers and the co-workers. I would like to work again, to get back into routine. They are wonderful hours, those working hours, sweating it out in the pursuit of happiness, feeling alive. How satisfying to bring home the kosher bacon, even though lots of fat is snipped off beforehand by payroll deductions. Yes, how wonderful it would be to participate once more in community projects, to be an alive active person, a citizen.

If you ever plan to take sick, be sure not to choose a Saturday or Sunday. These are the days when every single doctor in town makes it his business to go fishing or mountain climbing. Should you fall on either one of these two days and break a leg, you are left dangling between two bedsheets, just like the doctor who, at this precise moment, probably is dangling from a rope on some mountain ridge. Better put up a sign all over the house during the weekend, "Closed For Injury." I know this for sure because one of my bed neighbors was an eighty-four-year-old man who had the audacity to fall on a Saturday and it was not until 10:00 PM that night until either one of his two doctors could be reached.

Another warning: Don't get sick and old at the same time. That is too much of an affliction.

With my improvement, the desire to have a telephone at my bedside became more prevalent. Hello outside world! How are things? Please let me in on the party-line of living again. Life, here I come! Let us give each other a jingle.

I also moved into a private room which afforded me the luxury of listening to the good music station at 6:00 AM sans earphones. The Prince of Wales could not have been better off than I because now I had my private bungalow. I am able to turn on the lights anytime during the night without having to worry that I might disturb someone. When sleep avoids me, I can try to lure him while reading a good book.

An important moment fell into my life when I got "Kitty Hawk" off the ground for the first time. That is my by now most famous leg, which I was able to move a few inches off the bed under my own power. This apparently insignificant matter does become a major event in a situation like this. To raise a ghost could not have been a more jubilant affair than to bring my leg back under my own command. Hallelujah, praise the Lord!

A feeling of humbleness seems to come over me at this point. To be left alive in an accident which was very nearly fatal imposes a solemn duty. I have always felt that each one of us has a certain mission to perform, no matter how hazy this task might appear before us. My desire to write might be my mission or simply the expression of a sense of humor, to add a chuckle now and then. Who knows?

It is 6:00 AM, the usual time for me to jump out of bed, weekdays or Sundays, and work. Yes, a little matter like jumping out of bed is not my privilege at the present. Instead, I am nailed to the top of my bed. Luckily, my right leg can still serve as a desk against which I can lean my writing pad. While through the major part of my life I have been writing orders to manufacturers, I now order myself to write. It does not bring earthly goods in return, only inner satisfaction.

* * *

This is Valentine's Day. I never quite realized the beauty that some of these holidays have built into our calendar. Probably, I have never been the recipient of so many valentine cards before. It is really quite an interesting holiday devoted to love. You can send someone a valentine without actually becoming emotionally involved. It simply says, I like you; you stand out a bit and as far as I am concerned, I just want you to know. St. Valentine was a saint alright, whom we still recall by his saintly deeds and our often not quite so saintly remembrances.

My diary, I have neglected you a bit and I believe that it is due to my more rapid improvement. Activity of the brain seems to stand in opposite relation to physical activity. My knee muscles have strengthened to the point where I now raise my leg off the bed. I can also move from the prone position to the sitting-up position without the use of hands. It is a great feeling to see life return to my leg, even though the knee-bend is only a very slight one. On this, I will have to work over many months to come and go swimming and dancing (what a wonderful therapeutic prospect!) in order to get the muscles back into working condition.

The second X-ray was taken yesterday and it shows satisfactory progress. The screws and bolts are in place and some bone is forming around them, but not enough as yet to subject the limb to weight. On Monday, seven weeks after the accident, physical therapy will begin in true conformance with my point of view... from the horizontal to the vertical position. It is then when my glossary will find its end because the slant on things will become normal again, perpendicular rather than flat.

Hospital life goes on. Patients come and go. Today they brought in an honest-to-goodness Eskimo. She is elderly and broke one of her hips in a fall. Her fear was such from the moment she arrived that you could hear her scream all the way down the hall. She was admitted in the evening and when she let out with a lion's roar, the night nurses, a skeleton crew at best and also apparently not quite so well versed as the regular staff, were flying up and down the hall like swallows on their way to Vancouver, B.C. They were so rudely awakened from their nightly routine that they adopted more of the earmarks of migratory birds rather than homing pigeons. They finally stopped her wail, but I don't know to this day if it was done with a hypodermic needle or a mouth-plug. I report this incident because to me it was an interesting demonstration of the benefits of civilization, which, if nothing else, seems to guide fear into the channels of courage.

The most magnificent step forward, hypothetically speaking since I am still flat on my back with no chance of stepping out yet, is indeed physical therapy. The bubbling warm water into which I am lifted daily by means of a hoist, just like a case of dynamite, restores blood circulation. It gives an opportunity for leg movements and knee bending. Just as a twig will bend, so do our muscles.

* * *

Many things happened in the outside world while I was shut in and shut off from it. Yet, the radio and television brought occurances home to me. I could visualize the tremendous, deep valley in which humanity finds itself. Looking back, I realized that the present, no matter when, reflects deep shadow. There is a certain dampness, a coolness in the present time. Yet that present becomes the past and in glancing back, we see a lot of sunshine. We see successful efforts in climbing the mountain, realizations of which the present day, for some inexplicable reason, blinds us. The future too always looks bleak, but the future again turns into the past and only the sunny spots seem to be the ones we fondly remember. Therefore, eyeing the present time and the future in the light of the past, we realize that this is the only conclusion that one can draw...particularly from the horizontal position.

A certain trust in God, coupled with our own efforts to add at least an iota to the betterment of the condition in which we place the world, should give us trust that humanity will survive and yes, stride forward.

In my opinion, the most beautiful lines ever written in relation to what we call death are these:

From THANATOPSIS

By William Cullen Bryant

So live, that when they summons comes to join

The innumerable caravan, which moves

To that mysterious realm, where each shall take

His chamber in the silent halls of death,

Thou go not like the quarry-slave at night,

Scourged to his dungeon, but sustained and soothed

By an unfaltering trust, approach thy grave

Like one who wraps the drapery of his couch

About him, and lies down to pleasant dreams.

COSMOS

Heavy lies the dew upon young morning,
Like a mantle bestowed by demon night.
Darkness yields to world awakening,
So young, so fresh and so absorbing,
So bright, so full of vibrant rays.

Yawning, stretching, maybe even with a sigh,
All living matter girds itself for the daily task,
Bending with the wind or giving it battle,
Whatever its chosen goal, its interpretation,
A thread is an integral part of a woven picture,
All is substance, from the concrete to the Fata Morgana
In the sky.

Light and dark, shame or boldness,
In opposites lie Nature's wager,
Devout or heathen, ego or id,
Friction between two elements begets life's spark.
Hunger, yearning, desire to fulfill oneself,
Jet-propels the force of life.

This then is the explosive element made part of Man,
To pursue like a hunter and yet to be hunted,
By this pursuer, your own fixation.
Life and Death are like Olympic runners,
With stretched-out hand we impart the eternal flame
To those who are next,
Hoping that they will keep it burning,
That they will take it there where all beginning
Is end and where all end is just the beginning.